TANGO MIKE MIKE®

THE STORY OF
MASTER SERGEANT
ROY P. BENAVIDEZ

by

YVETTE BENAVIDEZ GARCIA

Photographs taken from the
Benavidez Family Archives

For more information on Roy P. Benavidez, visit the following sites:

www.roypbenavidez.wordpress.com
Facebook: Roy P. Benavidez, "Tango Mike Mike®"
You Tube: www.youtube.com/roypbenavideztangomikemike
Twitter: Yvette Benavidez Gar @ RoyPBenavidez
Instagram: www.instagram.com/roy_p_benavidez
Pinterest: www.pinterest.com/roypbenavideztangomikemike

DEDICATION

TO MY DAD, Roy. You truly are my hero. You always encouraged me to be the best that I could be, to be myself, and to never let what others say get me down. You always told me, "Yvette, you're OK. The world's wrong." Thank you, Dad. This one's for you.

To Ren, Ryan and Morgan. You've encouraged me every step of the way. Thank you for motivating me, always.

To my mom, Lala. You were always there when Dad couldn't be. Thank you for all of the sacrifices you made. You are an inspiration.

To all those who have daily crosses to carry. Be inspired and believe.

Finally, to the kids who are reading this book. My father dedicated his life to reaching out to those in school. He wanted every child to have the opportunity to finish school and to be the best that they could be. This book is for you. May you be inspired and encouraged to never give up.

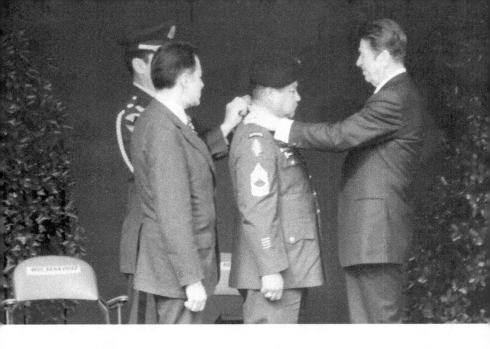

ROY P. BENAVIDEZ is a Medal of Honor recipient from El Campo, Texas. Most people call him a Medal of Honor "Winner," but he never liked that word. If he heard it said, he'd be quick to correct you and say he didn't WIN anything. You see, a winner is someone who wins something, as in a game or a sport. The medal that Roy received, he earned. He fought in a war and received it because he risked his life to save others. He is known among his military brothers as "Tango Mike Mike." The US military uses certain words to designate as call signs. "Tango Mike Mike," a nickname given to Roy by his brothers-in-arms, would translate into "That Mean Mexican." Although Roy was anything but mean. Roy was a soldier who went above and beyond the call of duty and voluntarily risked his life to retrieve classified documents and save the lives of others. His tenacious attitude, unstoppable drive and unyielding desire to save his comrades earned him the call sign, "Tango Mike Mike."

ROY WAS BORN on August 5, 1935, in a rural South Texas town named Lindenau. He and his younger brother, Roger, were born during a time when there was segregation and racism. Roy hated the fact that some people looked at the color of someone's skin, instead of red, white and blue — the colors of the American flag.

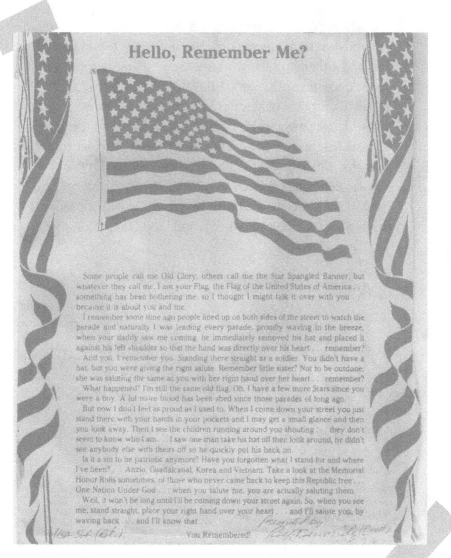

This was Roy's favorite poem. He had it memorized word for word and often ended his speeches with it. (Author unknown)

WHEN ROY WAS three years old, his father, Salvador Jr., got sick and died from tuberculosis. His mother, Teresa, remarried and had a daughter named Lupe. Four years later, she gave birth to another girl, named Bellatres, but she passed away at only six months of age. On September 25, 1946, when Roy was only eleven years old, his mother died from the same disease that took his father's life. This left Roy and his brother orphans. After the death of both of his parents, Roy's uncle, Nicolas Benavidez, offered to raise the two boys. His young sister, Lupe, stayed behind with her father. Roy's uncle moved the two boys to El Campo, Texas, and raised them as his own.

From left to right are Roy's uncle Nicolas and aunt Alexandria Benavidez, along with Roy and his wife, Lala, at their wedding reception. To the right are Lala's parents, Maria Hansen and Juan Coy. June 7, 1959.

This was the only picture Roy had of his mother, Teresa Perez Benavidez.

This photo, of Roy's parents (Salvador and Teresa Perez Benavidez) on their wedding day, was found in the Benavidez Family Archives after Roy had passed away. Unfortunately, Roy never got to see it.

YOUNG ROY HAD to earn his keep while living with his new family. He had nine new brothers and sisters, and life was not easy. Not only did he have to deal with the death of both of his parents, he now had to learn to live with and love a new family.

Roy earned extra money shining shoes, selling his aunt Alexandria's tacos, and helping the family pick cotton. He and his new brothers and sisters also spent their summers working in the fields and putting aside the little money that they made to help their parents.

ROY'S HARDSHIPS CONTINUED as a child. In fact, he left his hometown so often to pick cotton that he had to drop out of school. He was not proud of this, but at the time, he did not have a choice. Later in life, Roy would say in his speeches … "Like a fool, I dropped out of school." He always regretted this circumstance.

Growing up, Roy was not the perfect kid. He got into trouble a lot and he took to boxing to let out his frustrations. His uncle Nicolas spent many days at the school principal's office dealing with Roy's behavior.

Roy's uncle, Nicolas Benavidez, who raised and loved Roy as his own.

Roy at the age of fourteen.

THE RACISM AND segregation that Roy experienced didn't help his fighting attitude. It actually fueled the fire that was in Roy. There were times when Roy couldn't watch a movie in the local theater or sit in any seat that he wanted. There were signs that instructed all Blacks and Mexicans to go around and enter through the back and to sit up in the balcony. Similarly, restaurants had signs that said, "No Blacks or Mexicans allowed." Situations like this made Roy feel as if he wasn't worthy, but he never let that get him down. In fact, it was because of this that he wanted to better himself and make his aunt and uncle proud of him.

Sicily Drop Zone. Roy captioned this picture "Me coming in for a PLF," which stood for "Parachute Landing Fall."

Fort Benning, Georgia, Training Facility. This is where Roy trained to become a paratrooper.

IN 1952, WHEN Roy turned seventeen years old, he decided to join the Texas National Guard. This was his way of doing something good with his life. He believed that if he joined the military he could earn a better education and be trained for combat operations. He stayed in the Texas National Guard for three years. His real desire, however, was to join the Army and become a Green Beret.

EARLY IN HIS military career, Roy met a young, green-eyed Irish girl named Hilaria Coy. He affectionately called her "Lala" and began courting her. Lala's parents were very strict and did not allow Lala to see Roy without the supervision of her older brothers. Every time Roy wanted to take her out, one of her brothers had to go with them. Roy didn't mind her brothers tagging along, as long as he got to see Lala.

In 1958, Roy had to leave for Germany, but he continued to write Lala and send her pictures. Each picture that he sent would say, "To my one and only. With love and respect, Roy."

On June 7, 1959, while on leave from Germany, Roy married his "One and Only," Hilaria Coy.

WITH THE GREEN Berets heavily on his mind, Roy set out to become the best of the best. The Green Berets are commonly referred to as the Army's Special Forces. They are highly skilled operators, trainers and teachers. They are, indeed, the best of the best, and Roy was out to prove that he could be a part of this elite group of men.

Right before Roy's first tour in Vietnam, Lala gave Roy a medallion for him to wear. As Catholics, they believed in praying to the saints for intercession. Lala pinned a St. Christopher medal on Roy and prayed for his safe return.

November 20, 1965, Fort Bragg, North Carolina. Lala pins Roy with a St. Christopher Medal. St. Christopher is the Patron Saint of Travel.

The Men of the Green Beret

The men of the Green Beret are masters of their profession, the profession of arms.

Theirs is more than a job or an occupation. It is a way of life that requires a personal commitment found nowhere else in society. Its obligation is dedication...its demands, duty and loyalty...its principle, integrity...and its reward, personal satisfaction.

Their countrymen see them as the epitome of the American fighting man. Their badge of distinction is the green beret known and respected worldwide.

They wear it proudly!

This creed was found tucked away in one of Roy's scrapbooks. He proudly wore the Green Beret.

IN THE ARMY, Roy did two tours in Vietnam. During his first tour, he stepped on a land mine. The shock of the blast injured him so severely doctors said he was paralyzed. The explosion jolted his brain so violently that he wasn't expected to regain his senses, either.

Because of his injuries, he had to be flown to Brooke Army Medical Center in San Antonio, Texas. When he finally awoke, after days of being unconscious, the doctors told him that he would never walk again. He was, indeed, paralyzed from the waist down. He did not want to believe what the doctors were telling him. He wanted to prove them wrong.

During his stay, Roy's wife would visit him often, along with his brother Roger. Lala would bring him sandwiches from home as a special treat. However, Roy's hospital buddies would take his food to trick him. After weeks of this, Roy started asking Lala to put jalapeños in the sandwiches. The next time one of Roy's hospital buddies took a bite out of his sandwich, they got a fiery surprise. Roy did this to teach them a lesson: Don't take things that don't belong to you!

ROY'S RECOVERY WAS a long process. The staff at the hospital believed that he would never walk again, so their therapy was geared toward getting him ready to survive life without the use of his legs. Roy didn't like that, so he took his therapy into his own hands. Every night, he would drag himself out of bed and try to pull himself up against the wall in his hospital room. His roommates would make bets on whether he could do it. Roy did this type of self-therapy without the hospital staff or doctors knowing. After ten months of pure determination and hard work, Roy proved all of the doctors wrong and walked out of that hospital. His perseverance had paid off. He believed that he could do it, and he achieved it. Two years later, Roy trained and qualified to become the best of the best in the Army. He became a Green Beret.

Roy, before he earned the title Green Beret.

THE GREEN BERETS are the elite of the elite, as Roy always said. The qualifications, training and endurance are rigorous. Everything a Green Beret goes through in order to be the best of the best is tough, rugged and draining. Not only is it physically challenging, but it is mentally exhausting as well. Roy secured the distinction of being a Green Beret because he put his mind to it. Who would have ever thought that this son of a sharecropper and grade-school dropout would become part of such an elite group? If you really stop to think about it, how could this man who dropped out of school in the eighth grade study, train, and qualify for this group? How could someone qualify for the Green

Berets who had been told just a year previous that he'd never even walk again — that he'd be paralyzed from the waist down? How could someone who lived his life in physical pain endure the hardcore, labor-intensive training of the Special Forces? His faith, determination and positive attitude played an important role in him achieving his dream.

A moment of distinction for Roy as he proudly wears the Green Beret.

This is one of the actual medallions that Roy wore around his neck. Before he passed away, he gave it to his daughter, Yvette. In gratitude for St. Michael's protection over her father, she named her firstborn son after him —Ryan Michael Garcia. St. Michael has a special place in their hearts.

ON MAY 2, 1968, Roy, or Tango Mike Mike, was in Vietnam for a second time. He was in the jungles of Cambodia attending a church service when he overheard someone on a nearby radio calling in air strikes saying, "Get us out of here!" When Tango Mike Mike heard this call for help, without thinking twice, he quickly grabbed his bowie knife and a medic's bag. He made the sign of the cross and kissed his St. Michael medallion. St. Michael is the patron saint of paratroopers. Now that he was a Green Beret, Roy wore this medallion, too. Roy's devotion to his religion is what got him through his battles in life. He never wavered in his faith.

WITHOUT HESITATION, ROY voluntarily boarded a waiting helicopter. Roy went on this mission because he wanted to, not because he had to or because he was ordered to go. He wanted to go and save his buddies' lives.

Once the helicopter landed in the jungles of Vietnam, Roy jumped out and made it about 100 yards before he was hit by enemy fire. The blast from the gunfire knocked him back, but he got up. He made his way to the team of US soldiers who'd been pinned down by enemy fire and gave them medical care. He also formed a defense and rescue area and called in air strikes. His mission was to save his buddies and bring back classified documents that one of his comrades had. Despite being hit several times by gunshots, grenades and shrapnel, Tango Mike Mike spent six hours in the jungle of Cambodia that day fighting the enemy soldiers. Roy refused to abandon his efforts and would not leave until every man was out of harm's way.

Ultimately, he saved the lives of eight men. On board the helicopter were also several enemy soldiers. Roy later said, "I didn't want to leave anyone behind."

Roy had been clubbed, stabbed, bayoneted, shot and left for dead. His medical reports showed that he had sustained more than fifty-seven wounds to his head, face, neck, hands, arms, legs, back and buttocks. He was injured so badly that, when he was finally lifted onto the helicopter, he was holding his intestines in his hands. He was assumed dead because his injuries were so severe. Eventually, he would be placed into a body bag. As the medic was checking him over to confirm that he was indeed dead, Roy mustered enough strength to spit in the medic's face. That was the only way he could tell him that he was not dead: he was alive. Roy spent the next year undergoing several surgeries to repair all of his injuries.

Roy listens attentively as President Ronald Reagan reads the citation that retells Roy's six-hour mission.

ROY RECEIVED FOUR Purple Hearts as well as the Distinguished Service Cross for his duty that day. Years later, he would be recommended for the Medal of Honor, the highest award bestowed in the military for services performed above and beyond the call of duty.

However, he did not receive this award at that time. Even though he had saved the lives of eight men, there were no eyewitnesses who could attest to what Roy had done on May 2, 1968. The men who Roy had saved were sent to other hospitals for recovery, but Roy didn't know it. He thought they had died. Twelve years later, an eyewitness finally came forward and wrote a ten-page account of what had happened that day. The eyewitness' name was Brian O'Connor.

Brian O'Connor telephoned Roy twelve years after their mission and asked to speak to "Tango Mike Mike." Roy got emotional when he heard Brian's voice on the other end of the phone.

Brian and Roy at a Washington, DC, airport, the week Roy received the Medal of Honor.

The crowd numbered several thousand in the center courtyard of the Pentagon.

(Left to right) Denise, Yvette, Noel and Lala at the Medal of Honor Ceremony in Washington, DC. (February 24, 1981)

ON FEBRUARY 24, 1981, thirteen years after his 1968 mission in Vietnam, President Ronald Reagan awarded Master Sergeant Roy P. Benavidez the Medal of Honor. Departing from tradition, Reagan personally read Roy's citation before a crowd of thousands at the Pentagon in Washington, DC. Forty-one members of Roy's family were present to witness this momentous occasion. Before the President draped the medal around Roy's neck, he ended with these words, "A nation grateful to you, and to all of your comrades living and dead, awards you its highest symbol of gratitude for service above and beyond the call of duty, the Congressional Medal of Honor."

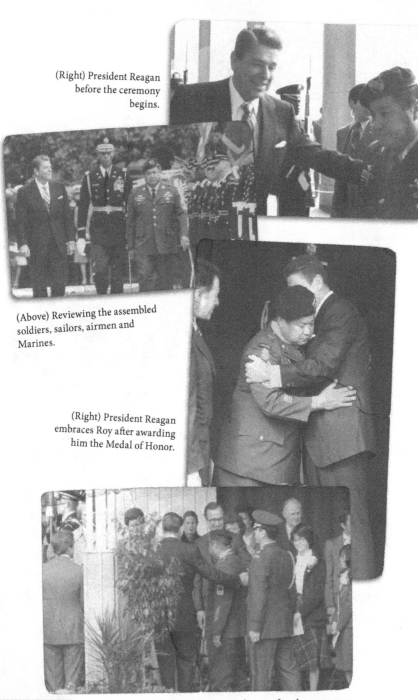

(Right) President Reagan before the ceremony begins.

(Above) Reviewing the assembled soldiers, sailors, airmen and Marines.

(Right) President Reagan embraces Roy after awarding him the Medal of Honor.

The family is escorted away after the ceremony.

Roy and his family on the steps of the White House.

AFTER ROY RECEIVED the medal, he traveled all over the world, speaking at schools, civic organizations, military institutes and Veterans hospitals. His mission was to motivate people to be the best that they could be. He wanted

Roy made it his mission to inspire students to stay in school and get an education.

everyone to know that, although he was deemed a hero, the heroes were the ones who never came home.

In his speeches, Roy talked about coming from a humble background where he had to work to get what he wanted. He spoke about helping his family out in times of need and overcoming a bad attitude about life, people and school to be the best that he could be. He talked about his faith and always putting God first in life. When he spoke to kids in schools, he ended his talks by urging them to stay out of gangs, stay off of drugs and continue their education. He wanted kids to never take things for granted — especially their parents, because he knew what it was like to not have his. He reinforced how a positive attitude will get you farther than ability. Since he was a grade-school dropout, he did not have a formal education. He educated himself by learning from others and by reading books. The more he read, the more he learned. Roy talked about never giving up, no matter what your circumstances in life.

Roy loved to visit his brothers-in-arms. Here he is visiting a VA Hospital during the Christmas season. (December 28, 1981)

ROY BENAVIDEZ PASSED away on November 29, 1998, at 1:33 pm in San Antonio, Texas, at Brooke Army Medical Center, due to complications of diabetes. His family was by his side. On December 4, 1998, he was buried at Fort Sam Houston National Cemetery in San Antonio, with full military honors. Hundreds of people were there to pay their final respects to a man who had given so much in his lifetime. He was only sixty-three years old.

ROY'S FAMILY

ROY'S WIFE, LALA, and their three children — Denise Benavidez Prochazka, Yvette Benavidez Garcia and Noel Benavidez — all live in El Campo, Texas, with their families. In all, Roy and Lala have eight grandchildren. They have seven grandsons and one granddaughter: Ben, Andrew, Matthew, Joe, Ryan, Jordan, Nicholas and Morgan.

(Right) Hilaria Coy Benavidez, Roy's wife. Roy affectionately called his wife "Lala."

(Above) The Benavidez Family, 1974.

(Left) Yvette Benavidez Garcia and family (Morgan, Ren and Ryan).

(Below) Denise Benavidez Prochazka and Stan.

(Above) Noel Benavidez and family (Matthew, Nicholas, Andrea and Jordan).

(Below) Andrew, Ben and Joe Prochazka.

SINCE HIS PASSING, Roy has received numerous awards posthumously. Many military and civic institutions now bear his name: The Roy P. Benavidez National Guard Armory in El Campo, Texas; a monument in Cuero, Texas; a con-

(Above) The USNS *Benavidez*, currently docked in Bremerton, Washington.

ference room at West Point; an Army Training Center in North Carolina; a Navy Cargo Ship christened the USNS *Benavidez*; a Community Park in Colorado; two elementary schools (in Houston, Texas, and San Antonio, Texas). In addition he has been the subject of several sculptures, four books and a Hasbro G.I. Joe Action Figure, just to name a few. Today, "Tango Mike Mike" is used in the military as part of their radio training. Soldiers are taught to use the call sign whenever there is trouble, or dire circumstances. Furthermore, if a firefight is going bad or courage needs to be summoned, a soldier will call out:

Tango Mike Mike
Tango Mike Mike

Roy's call sign.

(Right) Limited Edition Roy P. Benavidez G.I. Joe Action Figure.

ROY WAS ALWAYS asked, "If you had to do it all over again, would you risk your life to save your buddies?" His answer was always this:

"There will never be enough paper to print the money or enough gold in Fort Knox for me to have, to keep me from doing what I did. I'm proud to be an American and even prouder that I earned the privilege to wear the Green Beret. I live by the motto: Duty, Honor, Country."

CPSIA information can be obtained
at www.ICGtesting.com
Printed in the USA
LVHW091921061021
699707LV00008B/455/J

A Mystery at Lili villa

Arathi
MENON

A
MYSTERY
at **Lili**
villa

YALIBOOKS
NEW YORK

Published by Yali Books, New York

Text © 2021 by Arathi Menon
Cover Art by Shruti Prabhu

Connect with us online: yalibooks.com
Instagram / Twitter / Facebook: @yalibooks
Pinterest: @yali_books

Originally published in India as
A Thud in the Middle of the Night (Mango Books, 2019)

Published in agreement with DC Books, India

Library of Congress Control Number: 2021933668

ISBN: 978-1-949528-82-4

978-1-949528-81-7 (Paperback)/ 978-1-949528-80-0 (eBook)

Typeset in Adobe Text and Active

For the terrific three of my childhood—

Rekha, Suji & Radhi

Tam was spending the summer in Kerala with her cousins. On the first night of her vacation, she couldn't sleep. She lay awake in the silence of the night while the rest of the house slept.

Suddenly, she heard a loud THUD outside her window. Her heart nearly stopped. Then, she heard the sound of footsteps. They got louder and LOUDER. She shut her eyes tight and hugged Mira, who lay still, lost in dreamland.

When the sound of running feet seemed farther away, she cautiously opened her eyes. Nothing had changed. The room looked the same; their butterfly-shaped nightlight cast familiar shadows.

Stop! Stop! Stop! Begin at the beginning. Begin at the pooja.

ONE

A THUD IN THE MIDDLE OF THE NIGHT

"I hate poojas!" Tam screamed.

She tripped on the super long skirt she had been forced to wear. It was a pretty one, green with large gold dots, but Tam hated it. She missed her shorts.

Tam tumbled headfirst to the ground. She rolled and rolled and finally stopped at the feet of the priest. The pujari yelled, "Donkey!"

Tam glared at him. She would have stuck her tongue out, but Sheila Ammayi came running after her and stood there with her hands folded, her eyes beseeching Tam.

"Get up, get up, go back to the car," she whispered urgently.

Tam got on her feet. Everyone at the temple was looking at her. The priest quickly gave her family some prasad and prayed he wouldn't have to see them for a long time.

Sheila Ammayi closed her eyes and asked for patience while Damodar Ammavan's thick eyebrows danced on his crumpled forehead. Tam dragged herself toward the family car.

It was going to be a long summer.

Damodar Ammavan got into the driver's seat and thundered, "No dessert for you today! Don't you know how to behave at a temple?"

Tam's ammavan was unpredictable. He had yelled at her for half an hour for dropping a piece of cake, but when she and Arj had pushed the TV down in a fight—breaking it into a million pieces—he hadn't said a word. He even got them a newer, fancier TV the very next day.

Tam kept quiet. Arj and Mira turned around and winked, and Tam grinned at them. Of course, they would smuggle out some dessert for her. The cook, Pitamma, hated Damodar Ammavan. Every time the kids were punished, Pitamma would make the punishment lighter by bringing them some yummy food from her kitchen.

Half an hour later, they were home. Tam and Mira ran to Mira's bedroom and tore off their silk skirts and tops. Tam let out a long sigh. "Phoof! It's so hot in these things." The girls put on their shorts and tees and began to feel normal again.

Tam lived in Bengaluru and was visiting Elathoor for the summer. She loved Elathoor. Her cousins lived in a large white house called Lili Villa, surrounded by tall coconut trees. It had a front yard, two side yards, and a backyard dotted with mounds of mud that crumbled at a touch. Lili Villa was an old house with secret rooms, hidden passages, and cobwebbed corners. "It's the best place in the world to play hide-and-seek," Tam would boast to her envious friends back in Bengaluru.

Sheila Ammayi and Damodar Ammavan were both doctors. Everyone in the village knew them as they were the only doctors around. In Elathoor, if you got into an auto rickshaw and asked the driver to take you to "the doctor's house", you would come straight to Lili Villa.

Arj was already at the breakfast table. Temples made him hungry. Most things made him hungry. Breathing made him hungry.

They were having appam-stew for breakfast. Damodar Ammavan came in and sat down. Arj, Mira, and Tam immediately fell silent. The cook Pitamma walked in and banged a cauldron of potato stew and a stack of appams on the table. She was six foot, two inches tall and dressed like a man, in a tee with a collar and a lungi. Arj claimed he had seen her smoke a beedi behind the well. She wasn't someone you messed with.

Damodar Ammavan helped himself to three appams and hollered for a fried egg. Pitamma came in carrying five plates, each with a messy bullseye. Damodar Ammavan happily tore a piece of appam, dipped it in egg yolk, and popped it into his mouth. One by one, Tam, Mira, and Arj slowly slid their eggs to the floor. Whisko the cat, who was waiting for this moment, pounced on the three eggs. Not a trace of yolk remained. Whisko *loved* eggs.

After breakfast, the three of them ran out into the backyard.

"I need your help with my science project," Arj announced grandly.

Tam and Mira were curious; no scientist had ever asked for their help. Arj marched Mira and Tam to the farthest corner of the yard. There, lying in the sun, were strange, intricate machine parts. Tam bent down to pick one up.

Arj roared, "Don't touch anything, you clumsy cuckoo! They are all very delicate."

Tam glared at him, but she was too curious to argue. "What is it?"

"A motor. I am going to power it with a battery, and it will force water to gush out of this hole. It will be a miniature waterfall." Arj pointed at a hole in a tiny cave of mud.

He continued talking, but Tam and Mira had stopped listening. They Arj's mouth move like a goldfish: open, close, open, close. They kept nodding their heads, pretending to understand every word. Arj wasn't fooled. "Since you can't be scientists, you can be my assistants. Bring mud from that corner of the yard. We can use it to build a dam."

Tam was annoyed. "I am nobody's assistant. I don't want to carry mud!"

Mira dragged her away before she could pick a fight. At the other end of the yard, they picked up two coconut shells. They filled them with mud, placed them on their heads, and sashayed back to Arj.

"We have to be paid minimum wage."

Arj glared at Tam. What a troublemaker his cousin was. He pulled out two five-rupee coins from his pocket. "This is all I have."

Mira snatched the money. "We will put this in the piggy bank." She'd forgotten that she and Arj shared a piggy bank. Tam didn't care about the money. She didn't want Arj to get too comfortable playing chief scientist.

Soon, the dam began to take shape. At noon, Pitamma brought them a snack—raw mango slices dipped in chili powder, salt, and coconut oil. They stopped work and squatted on a mud mound, disrupting a highway of ants. The spicy-tangy mango made their mouths water. They finished eating quickly, licking the chili mixture off their fingers while watching squirrels run up the mango trees. Tam couldn't help thinking she was never this happy in Bengaluru.

After the break, Tam and Mira didn't want to work with mud.

Arj pleaded, "Don't be selfish. Think of science!"

"If you are so worried about science, why don't you carry the mud while we set up the motor?" Tam retorted.

Arj hastily changed his tune. "We will continue building tomorrow." There was no way he was going to let Tam near his precious motor.

It was going to be another two hours before lunch. Damodar Ammavan and Sheila Ammayi would return from the hospital and shower, and only then would lunch be served. Arj wondered if he should have a pre-lunch snack. His tummy gave a little growl on cue. Just then, his parents' white SUV drove into the yard. Luckily for Arj, they were early, and lunch would be served within the hour.

At Lili Villa, every meal was grand—four curries, two types of rice, yogurt, papadam, and pickles. Meals in Elathoor were feasts for Tam. At home in Bengaluru, she would only get one curry and one type of rice. She had asked her mum about the lack of curries once. "At Sheila Ammayi's home, Pitamma can cook up as many dishes as she likes. Here, you only have one overworked amma, so you have to be content with smaller feasts." Tam told herself that she would hire two cooks and enjoy six different curries and four rice dishes every day when she was older.

When lunch was finally served, Arj practically ran to the table. "I am so hungry I could eat Whisko." As if he understood, Whisko scooted from under the table and bolted toward the backyard. Damodar Ammavan walked in, and everyone stopped talking. They even chewed quietly. He didn't like conversation while they were eating. For some weird reason, he didn't approve of them sneezing at the table either. If any of them felt a sneeze coming, they would run out of the dining room and sneeze heartily, and only then return to the table. Once, Tam had sneezed at the table—Damodar Ammavan had just glared at her and walked away, leaving his half-eaten meal behind.

After lunch, it was too hot to play outside. Tam, Arj, and Mira ran up the stairs to their favorite hidey-hole: the top floor of Lili Villa. This part of the house was weird because the owner of the house had stopped construction midway. Arj and Tam would take turns walking on top of the half-finished walls like acrobats, with their arms stretched out, trying not to fall.

Someone had left a trunk full of comic books up there. They had discovered it one summer and made a pact not to tell the grown-ups. The old comics had superheroes with names they had never heard of: Mandrake, Phantom, Flash Gordon, Lothar, Bahadur.

Arj and Tam began to fight.

"I saw it first!"

"No, you didn't. I touched it first!"

They both wanted to read *Zam Zam's Circle of Death*. It had a fierce python on the cover, curled like a racetrack, with a skeleton riding a bike on its back. They were pulling at it, almost tearing it in half.

Mira yelled, "There's another copy. Don't fight!"

Arj and Tam grabbed a copy each while Mira continued to read an issue of Phantom. The only sound in the afternoon was the creaking of a table fan and the rustling of paper. Peace returned to the unfinished floor.

At five o'clock, Pitamma came around with tea and a snack. "Diamond cuts for my diamonds." She cackled. They grabbed handfuls of the sugar-coated, diamond-shaped biscuits. Mira popped one in her mouth. She liked it to melt and become a soggy clump before swallowing it whole.

The first day of their summer vacation was almost over. After a shower, the kids changed into their pajamas, and Pitamma served them dinner. They were tired by now, but they liked to wait for Damodar Ammavan and Sheila Ammayi to return from the clinic. The doctors sometimes brought home delicious treats they received from grateful patients. It was worth the wait—Ferrero Rocher chocolates from a first-time grandmother. Arj, Mira, and Tam stuffed their faces, and though they wanted to finish the box, they just couldn't. They were too full. Mira wandered off to give some of her chocolates to Pitamma. She was Pitamma's pet.

They wished the grown-ups goodnight and went to bed. Mira fell asleep first, and soon Tam heard Arj's heavy breathing.

Tam couldn't sleep. It usually took her two nights to get used to sleeping in a new place. She could hear dogs howling in the distance. When she was younger, Arj would frighten her. "That is the sound of wolves," he would whisper. "If you put your hand out of the window, they'll sneak up and bite your arm off. They'll come back for your other arm the night after." Even though Tam was ten now and was sure there were no wolves in Elathoor, she was still scared of sticking her hand out of the window. Wisely, she hid her fears from Arj.

Tam could sense that the whole house was asleep. She could almost feel the silence around her when, all of a sudden, she heard a loud THUD breaking the quiet of the night. Her heart nearly stopped. Then she listened to the sound of footsteps growing louder and LOUDER. She shut her eyes tight and hugged Mira, who lay still, lost in dreamland.

When the sound of running feet seemed farther away, she cautiously opened her eyes. Nothing had changed. The room looked the same; their butterfly-shaped night-light cast familiar shadows. She lay awake for a long time, wondering if the person with the loud footsteps would return.

TWO

FOOTPRINTS IN THE MUD

Tam woke up late the next morning. It was already eight o'clock, and she could hear Arj and Mira in the backyard laughing about something.

She smiled. "Sweet of them to let me sleep in. If only Amma could learn a thing or two from them." What she didn't know was that when they woke her up early, she turned into such a prickly-porcupiny-growly bear that nobody liked being around her. It was safer to let her snooze.

Tam stared at the ceiling, lazily wondering what the second day of vacation had in store for her, when suddenly she remembered the footsteps in the night. She felt a cold hand squeezing her heart, and her mouth turned dry.

Terrified, she looked around the room. *No strangers.* With her heart pounding in her chest, she forced herself to look under the bed. Two suitcases covered in dust and cobwebs looked back at her. *Could someone be hiding in those suitcases? No, of course not. Even I wouldn't fit in there.*

She leaped off the bed and ran toward the kitchen. As she flew through the musty corridor that connected the dining room and the kitchen, she imagined long, threatening shadows chasing her. She ran faster. Finally, she spotted Pitamma's starched lungi. She was safe. Pitamma could fight off anyone with her large muscular arms.

Tam took a seat on the wooden bench near the stove. She was too nervous to register that Pitamma was making her favorite, puttu-kadala. Pitamma stared at her, eyes bulging like white beetles. Without asking any questions, she banged a cup of hot black tea beside Tam. She clasped the glass tumbler and felt the warmth seeping into her hands. After a few sips, Tam felt her courage return. It was daytime, and if the person from last night was still around, they could call the police. Relieved, she went looking for Arj and Mira when she heard Sheila Ammayi call them for breakfast.

Tam could hardly eat. She was bursting with news, but she was too scared to share it with Damodar Ammavan's sharp eyes watching her. Sheila Ammayi noticed her lack of appetite. She touched Tam's forehead.

"Are you okay? It could be fatigue from your trip. Why don't you get some rest today?"

The doctors' driver entered the dining room and stood by the door. His name was K. O. Davis, but everyone called him Kodavis.

The children looked at him warily—they hated him. If they stood too close to him, he would pinch them so hard that it would leave a red mark. They didn't know how to tell the grown-ups about him, so they had learned to stay away. Arj had even signed up for karate classes to defend himself and Mira. Much to his disappointment, Arj's instructor had told him it would take him two years to learn how to knock down a man.

Kodavis leered at all of them and hello-helloed Tam. She ignored him; he could be the Footsteps Man. She would love to hand *him* over to the police.

Sheila Ammayi smiled apologetically at Kodavis. "Poor thing, she is tired," she explained and proceeded to give him instructions for the day.

Arj and Mira gulped down their breakfast and followed Tam into the backyard. She whispered, "Follow me!" and made a beeline for the farther corner of the yard, away from the grown-ups' ears. Once they reached the bottom of the yard, Tam spoke breathlessly, "I heard footsteps last night. Someone was prowling around the yard while you were sleeping."

"Could it have been a robber?" Mira asked nervously.

Arj sounded angry. "What? Why didn't you wake me up? I could have caught him."

Tam didn't want to confess that she'd been too scared to do anything, so she changed the topic.

"What should we do now?"

Arj knew this was too important to hide from his parents. "Let's tell Amma and Appa about it. They will call the police."

Tam nodded solemnly. "Yes. That's the best thing to do." Just then, they heard the car drive away. The doctors had left for the hospital.

"Should we wait till afternoon?" Mira asked. "When they are at the hospital, Amma said we mustn't disturb them unless it is an emergency. Should we message them? Is this an emergency?" They couldn't decide.

Arj finally thought it best not to risk annoying his parents. Instead, he announced, "We will make our own investigations and present our findings to Amma and Appa at lunch."

Tam and Mira agreed. How grand "investigations" sounded!

"I will be Chief Detective," declared Arj.

"No! I want to be Chief Detective. How come you get to be all the important people?"

Arj was skillful at handling his cousin. He asked, "Do you know what a detective does?"

"N-N-No-o," she stammered.

Arj smiled a superior smile. "Then how can you lead the team? I am eleven and the oldest. I will be Chief, and you can be my lieutenant."

"Fine, but I want to be Lieutenant Chief. I am ten now."

"Okay. Mira can be Junior Detective."

Mira didn't care what they called her as long as they let her join in. At nine, she was the baby, and she was always afraid they would leave her out of their exciting adventures.

Arj went into the house and returned with three floppy straw hats and a magnifying glass he pinched from his father's study. They put on their hats and immediately began feeling very detective-ish. Arj held the magnifying glass to his eye, making his eyeball look humongous. He struck what he believed was the right pose (folded hands, nose in the air) and said, "Detective work is all about logic. Logically, the first question we need to answer is: Why was someone in our yard last night?"

Lieutenant Chief and Junior Detective began guessing wildly, each wanting to be the one to give the correct answer.

"He wanted to steal the car."

"How do you know it was a 'he'?"

"He-she was practicing for the marathon."

"He-she wanted to hurt Damodar Ammavan because he couldn't cure them."

Tam whispered, "He-she dropped a body into the well." The three of them raced to the well. Nothing was floating on the surface. They knew from a zombie movie they had watched last year that a dead body floats in water unless you tied a heavy stone to it. Then it would sink. They peered into the well for a while when Tam had a thought. She whispered, "Dead bodies stink! After the heart stops beating, the cells begin to rot. Can you smell anything yucky?"

They stuck out their noses as far as they dared and sniffed. Whisko, who was sunning himself at the edge of the well, joined them in suspiciously smelling the air. Nothing. Bored, Whisko went back to his nap.

"Maybe he-she wanted to steal Gita, Rukmini, Laxmi, Parvati, and Shiva!"

Arj looked at Mira with new respect. "That's an excellent idea, Mira. Our cows are very valuable. They cost more than the car."

They ran as fast as they could to the cowshed.

Dumdumchechi, the lady who took care of the cows, was seated on an upturned milk pail, reading a magazine. She looked up at the children quizzically. They seemed a bit wired—wide-eyed and scared. She watched as they counted the cows. All her beloved animals were there, meditatively chewing their cud.

Arj collapsed on the mud floor. "As Chief Detective, I declare—no more running to find things. We'll walk. Detectives have to be secretive and quiet, not run around like trampling elephants."

Tam giggled. "You need to get fit, Chief Detective, or you will be fired from the job." Arj ignored her.

"Could it just have been Pitamma using the outside bathroom?" asked Mira.

Tam snapped. "Why would you think of the most boring explanation for this exciting mystery? You always say the wrong thing at the wrong time." But now that Mira had said it, they began to wonder if the person prowling around at night was in fact a murderer or a thief. It could have just been someone from the house walking to the bathroom.

Lili Villa had only one bathroom inside the house. The other bathroom was in the yard, and it was a bit of a walk from the main house to get to it. On some nights, they would watch Pitamma from their bedroom window, making her way with a flashlight: a solitary, brave figure striding in the blackness under the coconut trees.

Disappointed, like monkeys whose bananas had been snatched away, the three of them walked toward the bathroom. They had run out of ideas.

Tam piped up, "Follow me! Do as I do and do not ask questions. As Lieutenant Chief, I need to focus." She began walking around the house, looking intently at the ground.

Arj and Mira followed. They didn't know what they were doing or what they were supposed to find, but it seemed like fun. Arj used the magnifying glass and spotted a beedi packet buried in the mud, some insects on a morning stroll, and an old bottle of nail paint, whose red liquid had hardened and cracked.

Suddenly, Tam stopped. She pointed at the ground in front of her. There were two footprints, clearly visible in the soft mud. They looked up to see where they were. Mira held Tam's hand. It was right outside their bedroom window.

Arj muttered spookily, "Every contact leaves a trace." He practiced a slow karate move and immediately felt better. "Don't touch anything," he warned them and ran back into the house.

He emerged a few minutes later with a ruler, a notebook, and a pen. He bent down and measured the footprint—it was ten and a quarter inches long.

"Is that a large foot size?" Tam asked.

They measured their feet. Arj's foot was seven and a half inches long, while Tam's and Mira's measured five inches each. The intruder definitely had big feet.

Mira yelled, "There are more footprints up ahead!"

They began following them, feeling an odd mixture of excitement and fear. Where would they lead?

The footprints stopped abruptly outside Sheila Ammayi and Damodar Ammavan's room.

"It's almost as if he disappeared into thin air," said Arj, unable to keep the admiration out of his voice.

Tam scratched her head. "Humans can't disappear." Where could this thief/murderer/up-to-no-good person have gone?"

Mira squealed, "Maybe he-she is like Spiderman! He-she twisted their wrist, shot out a web, and climbed onto the roof!"

The kids looked up. The roof did have quite a few cobwebs. Arj poked Tam urgently and pointed at the wall below the tiles. Footprints could be seen going up to the very end and onto the roof.

"Junior Detective, climb up the mango tree and tell us what you see," Arj commanded Mira, the best climber among the three. When she got to the highest branch, she yelled, "Someone has taken a few tiles off! There is a hole in the roof just above Amma and Appa's bedroom."

Just then, they heard the car—the doctors were back. The children ran out to meet them. Damodar Ammavan was puzzled. Either something was wrong, or they wanted a big favor.

"Tam heard someone running in the middle of the night. We tried to solve the mystery. We found footprints outside our window leading to your room. Sorry, I took your magnifying glass without asking. Mira climbed a tree like a chimpanzee. I watched to make sure she didn't fall. Someone has taken the tiles off the roof." Words tumbled out of Arj in a gush of excitement.

Damodar Ammavan asked him to repeat the story, this time at a much slower pace. He turned to his wife. "Sheila, see if anything is missing."

A few minutes later, they heard a scream—"Aiiiiyaaaa!" It was Sheila Ammayi. Everyone rushed into her bedroom. The steel closet was open, and empty jewelry cases were strewn across the bed.

Sheila Ammayi was crying. "They have taken everything. All my jewelry!"

Damodar Ammavan patted her back. "Don't worry. Our family is safe; we can always replace the jewelry. Come, let's eat lunch first."

Tam was so surprised at Damodar Ammavan's calm response that she almost forgot about the burglary.

Everyone headed to the dining room. Damodar Ammavan asked Pitamma to serve them tea with lunch. This was unusual: tea was only served at four. Tam noticed that Damodar Ammavan hardly touched his meal. Pitamma eyed the somber party suspiciously, wondering whether her fish curry was a bit off.

Toward the end of the lunch, Thombu, the local policeman, barged in. Damodar Ammavan must have called him to report the burglary. Thombu and Damodar Ammavan had gone to the local school together and were best of friends.

Sub-Inspector Thombu's uniform was always tight, stretching over his belly. The buttons of his shirt looked ready to fly off. When not in uniform, he would wear tight colorful shirts, unbuttoned to the navel. No matter what he wore, he looked like a pregnant penguin. With his stomach leading the way, Thombu walked up to Damodar Ammavan and fiercely clasped his friend's hand.

"Don't worry, Damu. We will get the thugs who did this."

Seeing him, Sheila Ammayi began to cry again. Mira hugged her mother. Tam rolled her eyes and whispered to Arj, "Can't they start the investigation? All this drama is such a waste of time."

First, the sub-inspector inspected the hole in the roof of the bedroom.

Sheila Ammayi sniffled. "The closet doors were closed when I woke up in the morning. I didn't think anything was wrong."

"Didn't you notice the tiles missing from the roof?"

"Nobody walks around looking at the roof. I'll fall and break my neck if I do that. Who will look after the children then?" Sheila Ammayi snapped at him.

Thombu hastily retreated. "You are right. After all, how many times a day do we look up at the ceiling?"

Damodar Ammavan whispered to Thombu, "She's upset. She didn't mean to be rude."

Thombu nodded and marched into the yard to examine the set of footprints. He took out a measuring tape and measured each print, making a note of it in a book.

"Just like me," whispered Arj, proud of himself.

Thombu also took photographs of everything with his phone. Still a bit scared of Sheila Ammayi's temper, he whispered to Damodar Ammavan, "This new phone is very good for photos."

Damodar Ammavan nodded. He understood his friend's pride. There had been a time when neither of them could afford to buy even a cold drink.

Thombu asked in a sharp voice, "Do you suspect anyone on your staff?"

Damodar Ammavan shook his head. "Everyone here has worked for us for years. I trust them completely."

Thombu snorted, "That may be true. But I still have to question them." He turned to Arj. "Gather everyone who works here at Lili Villa. Tell them Sub-Inspector Thombu wants to have a chat with them."

Arj gave a detective-ish nod and walked toward the kitchen with Mira and Tam following him. They summoned Pitamma first, then Dumdumchechi, and finally Kodavis.

Once the staff had assembled, Thombu pompously announced, "Stand in line, please. One by one, place your foot next to the first footprint. I need to measure your shoe size."

Kodavis was first. Much to the thrill of the children, his foot was an exact match. Kodavis immediately protested, "No! This can't be right. I swear, I swear on my mother,

I swear on the children, I swear on Sheila Madam, I am innocent. That is not my footprint." Thombu glared at him and said, "Damodar, keep an eye on that fellow."

Dumdumchechi was next. Her footprint matched as well.

Kodavis immediately relaxed and sneered, "She is always here before anyone wakes up. Who knows what she is doing during that time?"

Finally, it was Pitamma's turn. She was furious that she was being considered a suspect and lashed out, "Why is the staff being investigated? Maybe the family has stolen the gold for insurance money. I saw a case like that on TV."

Irritated by her comment, Damodar Ammavan picked up his squeaky-clean chappal and placed it next to the indentation. It was an exact match.

Sheila Ammayi slid her slipper in next. Luckily, it was three sizes too small. The kids all had a go, which was great fun, but they already knew their shoe sizes wouldn't be a match.

Satisfied, Thombu declared, "Good. This is enough information to file a report."

As he was leaving, Pitamma called out, "Let's see if your shoe fits. You were at the house yesterday, weren't you, complaining of a stomachache?"

Thombu was clearly angry, but he couldn't say anything.

He knew Pitamma's son worked for a local news channel and could create trouble for the police. He took off his shiny black shoe and, grumbling under his breath, placed it next to the shoe print. The children tried hard to stifle their giggles. The policeman and the thief could swap boots.

Tam voiced what was running through everyone's mind. "This is completely bonkers! Damodar Ammavan, Thombu, Pitamma, Dumdumchechi, and Kodavis all have the same shoe size—ten and a quarter inches! Who could the thief possibly be?"

THREE

EVEN YOU ARE A SUSPECT

Before he left, Thombu gave the family some homework.

"Think carefully. Write down the names of people who visit the house regularly. Don't leave anyone out. Even if you like the person, even if that person is your best friend, and you know in your hearts that they would never steal, write down their name. Everyone is a suspect until proven innocent."

Even you, thought Tam darkly.

The family gathered around the dining room table and began compiling a list of suspects. Sheila Ammayi wrote it down in her neat handwriting.

DoubleMean (No one knew her real name. She was the fish lady who came by every day at half past nine in the morning. Only Pitamma interacted with her—buying freshly caught crabs, mackerel, prawns, and Damodar Ammavan's favorite fish, pearl-spot. The kids called her DoubleMean because she never gave Whisko any fish. No matter how mean she was to the cat, he would always rub his head affectionately against her leg.)

Kodavis (K. O. Davis or Kodavis was the driver. He had been with the family for two years. The kids hated him because of his pinching fingers. Damodar Ammavan wasn't too fond of him either. Arj had overheard him tell Sheila Ammayi, "He has shifty eyes. I don't trust him." He was, however, an excellent driver.)

Dumdumchechi (She was the lady who took care of the cows. She was the heaviest person in the village, almost four times the size of the hole in the roof. No one knew when Dumdumchechi came to the house every morning. She was there before anyone was awake, and no one ever saw her leave.)

Fan-Fixer Faekku (He was the local electrician. He had come to fix a slow-moving fan in Sheila Ammayi's bedroom on the day of the burglary. He fixed the problem but created a new one: the fan now made an awful racket.)

Damodar Ammavan and Sheila Ammayi ruled out their patients. All of them were seriously ill—one had a case of measles, two of chickenpox, three of chikungunya fever, and one was suspected to be suffering from pneumonia—and were sent to the hospital immediately. Damodar Ammavan remarked, "If they can't even walk, how can they scale walls?"

Tam suddenly yelled, "The well cleaner! Well-Cleaner Mani!" Everyone was impressed. He was at Lili Villa the day before the burglary to scrub green moss off the walls of the well.

"If he can descend fifty-four feet into the well, he can climb up walls too. I'll put his name down," said Sheila Ammayi.

Since she had thought of Well-Cleaner Mani, Tam was convinced he was the thief. In her head, she had already proven his guilt and put him behind bars.

Mira whispered in a small voice, "I don't believe Taramma will steal from us."

Everyone turned to look at her. Taramma was their favorite visitor; she was a retired nurse and a friend of the family. Sheila Ammayi and the kids adored her. She would come by every third or fourth day, bringing the children treats from her house. She had dropped in on the day of the burglary with cashew fruit. She was the kindest, sweetest person in the village.

Damodar Ammavan's eyebrows chased each other like earthworms. He liked her too. "She is probably innocent, but we have to add her name to the list."

Arj was feeling a little left out and began furiously thinking of a suspect. Suddenly, he hollered, "Veer Sagar!"

The doctors nodded. Veer Sagar was a strange man. He was built like a wrestler—very fit and very strong. He didn't seem to hold a job, but he was never short of money. The villagers would often find him prowling around other people's homes. When asked, he would have a flimsy excuse at the ready. He lived alone and had no friends or family. If you asked him where he was from, he would mutter mysteriously, "Near Delhi." Once, Damodar Ammavan had gotten irritated and snapped, "Even Kashmir is close to Delhi compared to Kerala!"

On the day of the burglary, Pitamma had found him on the top floor of Lili Villa, snooping through the comics in the trunk. She had sneaked up on him and had shouted in his ear, "Fish fry!" He had shot up in the air, frightened out of his wits, and had run out of the gate at full speed. If you wanted to see Pitamma laugh with her stomach jiggling, spitting little bits of paan, you just had to yell "fish fry" and pretend to run like your bottom was on fire.

They couldn't think of any more names. Everyone stared at the list written in neat black letters. It was horrible to think that someone they knew walked into their house and stole something. Tam felt a bit frightened to see the names so clearly spelled out. It looked as if the suspects would leap off the page.

List of Suspects for the Burglary Committed on May 12th

1) **DoubleMean**

2) **Kodavis**

3) **Dumdumchechi**

4) **Fan-Fixer Faekku**

5) **Well-Cleaner Mani**

6) **Taramma**

7) **Veer Sagar**

8) **Pitamma**

Tam mentally added Damodar Ammavan and Thombu to the list. *Their foot size had matched too*, she thought. *Detectives shouldn't be sentimental.* In a rare show of wisdom, she decided not to insist on putting their names down.

Arj begged his parents, "Can we have the tablet and phone, please?"

It was an unwritten rule that summer holidays had to be gadget-free. No phones, no tablets, not even video games. Of course, the grown-ups still used their smartphones and computers.

Arj added in an official-sounding voice, "We need it for research, to find out more about each suspect, and solve the crime."

Tam and Mira were most impressed. They would have immediately given this Chief Detective whatever he needed to solve the case.

Much to their disappointment, Sheila Ammayi used her stern voice. "This isn't something for children to solve. The police will handle it. Forget about what happened. Go and play." The kids knew that voice. It meant no amount of begging would work.

Feeling dejected, the newly minted detectives wondered what to do next when Tam thought of something. "Sherlock Holmes, the world's greatest detective, didn't have a tablet or a smartphone, but he managed to solve more than a zillion cases. We only need our brains to find the thief."

Chief Detective and Junior Detective cheered up. They were going to solve this mystery the old-fashioned way.

FOUR

MORPH INTO A DETECTIVE IN THREE EASY STEPS

1) UNDERSTAND WHAT AN ALIBI MEANS

2) TURN TWO BIKES INTO THREE

3) THROW YOUR PARENTS OFF THE TRACK

Pitamma frightened Arj by creeping up and plopping a plate of peeled jackfruit next to him. The smell of jackfruit was strong and heady, and flies began circling overhead. The kids attacked the fruit, trying to gobble up more than their share.

Tam and Mira were goofing around when Arj shushed them. Tam looked around. *Was the burglar back?* Mira tried to hold Tam's hand and received a sharp whack.

Arj tiptoed to a spot right below an open window in Damodar Ammavan's consulting room. They could hear Thombu's voice loud and clear, as if they were inside the room. "I am going to investigate each suspect. If any one of them does not have an alibi for the night of the twelfth,

I will take him or her in for questioning. Don't worry, Damu. I will catch the criminal."

Damodar Ammavan replied, his voice soft and a little sad, "Question the staff at Lili Villa last. I don't believe they are thieves, and I don't want to upset them. I trust them with my children. What could be more precious?"

They heard Thombu's boots walking away and a door bang shut. Arj turned around and tiptoed back to the jackfruit, with Tam and Mira in tow.

As soon as they were far enough from the consulting room, Mira demanded to know what an "alibi" was. Arj wished he had his tablet. A simple search on it would have given him a million answers in less than a second.

Luckily, Tam knew this one and puffed up with importance. "An alibi is proof that a person was somewhere else when a crime was committed. For example, if Mira were killed—"

"Why me?"

"And Arj was one of the suspects—"

"Why me!"

"Then all Arj has to do to prove his innocence is to claim he was playing chess with Sheila Ammayi at the exact time of the murder. He couldn't possibly be in two places at once. Sheila Ammayi would have to confirm that Arj was with her. In this example, Arj's alibi is Sheila Ammayi."

Mira still looked a bit puzzled, but Arj was excited. "Fantastic! That means we will have to find out what our suspects were doing on the twelfth. If any of them are unable to provide us with an alibi for that night, they might be our thief."

Mira tried exaggerating her puzzled look. Tam and Arj ignored her.

"How do we do that?"

Arj had the answer. "We will have to start our investigation. Turn up at these people's houses, speak to them, maybe even question their neighbors."

Tam could hardly breathe. This summer vacation was turning out to be wild.

Mira, who finally understood what was happening, whined, "We only have the two bikes, and I am NOT going to be left out."

"Dang! My bike is at home in Bengaluru. Should I ask Amma to mail it? Can you even mail a bike?" No one knew for sure. What they did know was that Tam's mum wouldn't waste money sending a bike all the way from Bengaluru.

Arj had a brainwave. "Kodavis leaves his bike in the shed every morning and only comes back for it at night. Maybe we could borrow it from him?"

Tam refused. "I am not going to ask that horrid pincher for anything."

Arj knew it would have to be him.

The following day, Arj put on two tees, a shirt, and two sweaters. He looked ridiculous.

At the cowshed, he saw Kodavis leaning against the wall and reading a newspaper.

"May I borrow your bike during the day when you are out driving?"

Kodavis sneered. He put his arm around Arj's shoulders in a seemingly friendly gesture. Then he tried to pinch him, but Arj's arm felt strange. He couldn't feel any flesh. Instead, his pinching fingers kept clutching at some lumpy fabric. This confused him a bit. Disappointed, he curtly replied, "Okay. But if anything happens to the bike, your father will have to pay for the repairs."

Arj hurried back to his room and threw himself on the bed, laughing. He couldn't wait to tell Mira and Tam. Evil Kodavis had met his match.

Arj called for a meeting.

"We can't begin investigating right away."

Tam tried to object. "Why do we have to wait? A detective knows that any delay would give the thief more time to escape."

Arj looked stern. "We have already been told this isn't something for us to solve. Do you want Amma-Appa to ban our investigation and insist we stay at home all the time?" Tam was quiet. Arj made perfect sense.

He continued, "I have a plan. For the next two days, we will have to pretend that we have a newfound interest in biking. Once Amma and Appa get used to the idea of us leaving the house every day, we will get to work."

Digging into steaming hot puttu and spicy brown kadala at breakfast the next morning, Arj brought it up as casually as he could.

"We are thinking of biking around Elathoor. It's good exercise, and Tam can see more of the village."

Sheila Ammayi, who was always ready to spot a weak link in any plan, demanded, "How will the three of you ride two bikes?"

"I asked Kodavis if I could borrow his Zero, and Tam can use mine."

"No son of mine will ride around on a Zero."

"Why not?" asked an irritated Damodar Ammavan. "What is wrong with a Zero? When I was young, that's what everyone rode, not these fancy fifty-gear bikes."

Sheila Ammayi reluctantly agreed. When Damodar Ammavan went off on a "when I was young" tangent, there was no reasoning with him. She switched gears and quizzed them on their plans instead.

"Where will you go?"

"The Promenade."

"Okay. Be careful. Take care of Tam. Remember, she doesn't know the place."

Hah! Tam thought. *I can take care of myself, thank you.*

The doctors left for work. The kids trooped to the bikes parked in the garage. They were about to get on and ride away when Pitamma came running and dropped a package into Mira's bicycle basket. She wiped the sweat off her face, flashed a bright red paan-stained smile, and waved them on.

The Promenade was a picturesque stretch of road that ran alongside the river. A local professor won an international award for a book he wrote, and he spent the prize money on building something beautiful for the entire village to use. He was respected and well loved in Elathoor.

In the evening, the Promenade was packed with people—young couples, mothers with babies, old folks—taking in the beauty of the river, momentarily forgetting the worries of daily life. Street vendors appeared after four o'clock, hawking all kinds of things to eat, just when the crowd was hungry and ready to spend their money.

Tam, Mira, and Arj reached the Promenade in under twenty minutes and parked their bikes. It was quiet in the morning. They sat on a bench under a shady banyan tree and listened to the gurgling of the river water. Tam sighed.

"This is so boring. When does the action begin?"

Arj gave her a superior smile. "Detective work requires a lot of patience. If you don't have it, you are welcome to stay at home."

This made Tam furious. She stormed off for a walk around the Promenade. Mira ran after her; she was bored too. Arj stayed put on the bench, staring at the river and thinking of river-fish curry.

After a couple of hours, Arj was predictably hungry. He tore open Pitamma's package. She had packed orange marmalade sandwiches, three green apples, and three pieces of brown jaggery. Once the girls returned from their walk, the three of them polished off the food and headed home. It was nearly time for the next meal.

At lunch, Sheila Ammayi and Damodar Ammavan asked them about their trip to the Promenade. The children rattled off a bunch of facts with feigned enthusiasm.

"We saw a hundred-year-old tree."

"A stone engraving detailed the history of Elathoor. The village is named after a river and means 'the eyebrow of the sea'."

"We learned to tell time with a sundial."

The grown-ups were impressed and thought biking was proving to be a knowledge-building activity.

Arj didn't ask for permission the following day. As soon as the doctors left for work, they got on their bikes and rode to Elathoor Library.

They spent two hours reading the most boring books ever written. They also caught the eye of at least six of Damodar Ammavan's patients, all of whom could be relied upon to call the doctor to say they had spotted his kids at the library. It was a small place, and people talked.

At lunch, Damodar Ammavan confirmed it. "My friend Madhav Mash said he saw you three in the library. I hope you found something of interest to read. The library has a lot of rare and wonderful books. I used to spend hours there."

The kids nodded eagerly. Sheila Ammayi didn't quiz them any farther, and Arj sighed in relief. This meant they could now bike around the village and even if people spotted them, Damodar Ammavan and Sheila Ammayi wouldn't be suspicious. No questions would be asked, and no lies would have to be told.

After lunch, the three of them huddled together in their bedroom. Arj whispered, "Here's the plan—starting tomorrow, we will go through the list of suspects one by one, crossing them off our list if we discover that they have an alibi. I think we should take Appa's advice and investigate those at home last."

Tam called his bluff. "You want to investigate Pitamma last because you are afraid that if we question her, she will get angry with us and stop giving us her yummy food."

Mira giggled. "You're right, Tam. Arj hates to upset Pitamma."

Arj ignored them. "Let's investigate DoubleMean first. I saw her at the fish market yesterday; I know exactly where to find her."

The girls agreed. All of them felt a strange sensation in their stomach: a mix of excitement, fear, and anticipation. They could finally begin their detective work without the fear of detection.

FIVE

IS DOUBLEMEAN REALLY MEAN?

Tam was late again. It was already nine o'clock in the morning. She rushed out of the room to find Arj and Mira waiting for her, ready to begin their investigation. In super quick time, as if she were on fast forward, she washed up, brushed her teeth, showered, gulped down breakfast, and was all set to go.

Mira sniffed Tam's arm. "How do you shower in less than three minutes? Did you use soap?" She could never understand how Tam could wash up so quickly. At least she wasn't stinky.

They got on their bikes and pedaled as fast as they could to the fish market. They were unusually silent, their hearts hammering under their skin. It was their very first day as detectives. The sky seemed bluer, the air crisper. They had this unshakable faith that something exciting was about to happen.

They could smell the fish market before they could even see it. They parked their bikes outside and went in. Tam wrinkled her nose. "Phoof! Dead fish stink like socks that have been worn for a hundred years!"

Everything, even the dogs, smelled of fish. Their ticks probably smelled fishy too.

Fisherwomen had laid out the fish for sale in neat rows, packed in ice. Tam touched one of them. Their skin felt cold, unlike in the hot fish curry Pitamma made. Some of their eyes were red and, since they didn't have eyelids, they seemed to be icily staring at the people who wanted to buy them. The fisherwomen and their customers were yelling at the top of their voices, haggling over the price. It reminded Mira of how her class sounded when the teacher left the room.

They walked around looking for DoubleMean.

"See? The smaller fish are displayed in the outer circle, while the bigger ones are in the inner circle, closer to the center of the market," Tam pointed out.

There were cats everywhere, each a patchwork of colors. Mira kept getting distracted because she just *had* to pet every one of them.

Arj was an authority on fish. He would look at a specimen and declare it to be a white pomfret or black something or other. As he walked through the aisles, he would mutter under his breath, "Mackerel, sole, sardine. . ."

He knew all sorts of fishy names. Tam and Mira had no clue what the fish were called, so they couldn't tell if he was referring to them by the right word. He could call a long-tailed eel a "bambooska", and the girls wouldn't know the difference.

At one point, Arj crouched down and showed Tam and Mira how to check for freshness.

"The skin should glisten. If you press the fish's flesh, it should spring back." Then he gave them another gross tip. "Lift the flap covering the gills and see if the blood looks fresh."

"Yuck!" Mira was horrified.

Tam pretended to lift Mira's ear to see if she was "fresh". Before Mira could object, she heard someone calling her name. It was DoubleMean. She had spotted the children and was waving frantically. She didn't want them to buy from anybody else; they were her children.

They walked toward her. Whenever Tam or Arj needed the grown-ups to do something for them, they would get Mira to ask. They claimed she was the cutest. As planned, Mira pulled out her notebook. "Hello, chechi. I have to complete a summer project for school, and I have chosen the fish market as my topic. Can you help me by telling me how this market works?" This was true. Mira did have to write about her summer vacation.

DoubleMean beamed. "Of course. You can write about me and then I will be famous at your school. Ha, ha, ha!"

A cat came along and rubbed his neck against DoubleMean's ankle. She instinctively dug into a dirty plastic bag next to her and came up with some slithery, slimy, weird fishy parts. She tossed them at the cat as the kids watched in disgust.

DoubleMean began complaining about Pitamma. "Your Pitamma is so cruel. She never lets me feed poor Whisko. I think it's because she is jealous. She is very possessive of that cat. But I don't care about what she thinks. I feed Whisko some leftover bits once I am outside the gate. I think he loves me more than Pitamma."

Mira whispered to Tam, "Mystery solved. That's why Whisko adores her."

The three detectives spent the next two hours sitting cross-legged at DoubleMean's fish stall. They watched her haggle with customers. *Always quote double the price, and never go below half the quoted price.* They learned how to clean and gut fish. *Hold the fish with confidence. Babies and fish must be held firmly, or they will slip. Scrape the scales, insert the knife blade just below the head, and slide the tip till you reach the backbone. Cut along the bone till you hit the tail. Flip the fish over, repeat on the other side. Finally, clean the waste near the tail. There. Your fish is ready to cook. Want an easy fish fry recipe?* They jotted down a recipe and found out which parts were best to feed cats.

DoubleMean was a mean multitasker—gutting, haggling, and bagging fish, and talking nonstop. Toward the end, the detectives' heads were spinning with all the new facts they had learned.

By half past eleven, DoubleMean had sold most of her fish. "You three are my lucky charms. I have never sold all my fish by noon. Why don't you come by every day? I will give you a commission of 20 percent. Ha, ha, ha!"

The kids smiled politely. They still hadn't figured out how to bring up the burglary. They didn't want to seem rude, but all DoubleMean wanted to talk about was fish. She was busy packing up when they spotted a tall, very fit man sporting a blue-pink lungi. A colorful handkerchief was knotted on his head. He was quietly watching them.

DoubleMean beamed at the man. "This is Kannan. He is the best fisherman in Elathoor, and my husband." She introduced the kids.

Kannan grinned at them. "Have you ever been on a fishing boat? Would you like to go on a fishing trip?"

Arj couldn't believe their luck. "Really? Of course!"

After a ten-minute walk, the five of them were at the beach.

Parked in the sand was a beautiful blue boat with the word "Kalucia" painted on its side in large yellow letters. That's when they found out that DoubleMean's name was Lucia, and the boat was named after the couple: Kannan + Lucia = Kalucia.

"Our old boat was destroyed in a storm. We had to save for five years to buy this one. It's almost brand new, just about a month old. It has a diesel motor, see? Hopefully, there won't be a storm like that again, and this boat will last till Lucia turns into an old woman, but you never know." With these cheerful words, the fisherman invited the children to help him pull the boat out to sea. All five of them tugged at two long ropes attached to the hull. The boat skidded in fits and bursts over the sand, and when it hit the water, it began gently bobbing in the sea. The detectives stared at the boat, moved by the scene. It was almost as if they had helped it swim. What felt like a block of stone was now floating, light as a feather.

They got in. Kannan, Tam, and Mira sat on one side, while Arj and DoubleMean perched on the other end to balance the weight. Kannan barked out instructions, smiling the whole time, his white teeth glinting in the sunlight. "Don't make any sudden movements. Don't stand up or sit down without asking. If you need anything, raise your hand. If we are not careful, the boat can overturn, and then you will have to swim in the sea with the sharks."

Kannan started the small motor. It was horribly loud; they couldn't even talk to each other while it was running. Arj, on the other hand, was secretly relieved he didn't have to row. After half an hour, Kannan cut the motor, and silence surrounded them—a huge relief to their ears. They were now in the middle of the ocean. The kids looked around the endless blue, feeling like there was no one else in the world: just the five of them, a boat, and the afternoon sun. Kannan and DoubleMean smiled. They knew the effect the ocean had on someone experiencing it for the first time.

Kannan brought out a large fishing net and threw it over the side. "Fishing is part luck and part skill. I have the skill, and Lucia is my luck."

DoubleMean blushed. "It was on a clear day like this that we fell in love. My father had taken me on my first fishing trip. I was walking on the boat deck when I slipped on some fish guts and fell. I wasn't hurt, but one of my sandals flew overboard. My father asked me to check with the other fishermen that evening, in case the sandal had been snagged in one of their nets."

Kannan beamed. "My net had caught her pretty sandal, green with pink flowers—"

"He said he would give it back only if I went on a boat ride with him. I was nervous, but I had to go. Those sandals were the only pair of footwear I had," DoubleMean interrupted.

Kannan burst out laughing. "She saw the way I caught fish that day, and she got caught in my net, too."

DoubleMean offered them some dried fish and roti. They forced themselves to eat it despite the smell, feeling the salt tingling on their tongues.

Kannan sang–

The fish dash and dart,

But the fisherman's smart.

They'll swim into his trap,

He'll catch them in a snap!

Natholi fry or pomfret curry?

The fisherman's coming, hurry, hurry!

He continued in Malayalam but they couldn't quite catch the words. Arj was impressed. Even his appa couldn't sing a song in English.

Soon, the three of them began to feel sleepy. The kids had started to doze off when they felt a great movement under the boat. The word "capsized" flashed in Arj's head, and he looked at Mira. Luckily, all three of them had learned to swim the previous summer.

Kannan wasn't worried at all. He began expertly pulling the net up. "I think I got a big one."

The catch came up over the water, and they saw an enormous fish struggling to escape. It was over three feet long and had silver-red scales. Parts of its skin shimmered like a seashell—a mangrove jack. Kannan carefully dropped the net into a compartment at the bottom of the boat, filled with water to keep the fish alive and fresh. He then scooped out all the little fish caught in the net and returned them to the ocean. He explained to the puzzled children, "The big one is enough for us. We must not be greedy, or the Sea Mother will be very angry."

They watched the big fish for a long time. He stopped struggling and lay quietly in the water. Tam felt a bit sorry for him. "Maybe he is saying goodbye to life and preparing to become fish curry."

Kannan had saved five tiny fish for them. He handed them over to DoubleMean, who pulled out a little stove, and fried fresh fish in some fiery red masala in the middle of the ocean. She probably used the recipe she had given them earlier, but the kids couldn't be sure.

The fish melted in their mouths. Arj licked his lips. "This is the best fry I have ever eaten."

DoubleMean cackled loudly and squealed, "Don't tell Pitamma! You know how jealous she is. She will ask me to stop coming to the house."

They began heading back after the impromptu meal when Kannan pointed to a spot far in the distance. "That's your house."

The kids craned their necks to see, almost falling into the water in the process.

"I can see Lili Villa's roof! I am sure that's the one," Mira shouted. Arj and Tam couldn't tell; all the roofs looked alike.

"I heard about the burglary," said Kannan. "Lucia and I were on the boat the night of the burglary, right around here. We were catching catfish, which only come out at night. If I had a pair of binoculars that night, I could have spotted the burglar." He then became angry, "Whoever stole from the good doctors should be in jail." Arj glowed with pride, thinking of how much the village folk loved his father.

Tam hissed, "Alibi!"

DoubleMean couldn't have been the thief if she had been on the boat with Kannan on the night of the burglary. Their first suspect turned out to be innocent, but they were glad. They had had such a great time with Lucia and Kannan. It would have been horrible if they'd ended up handing them over to Thombu. The detectives helped pull the boat back onto shore and thanked the couple for a terrific day.

Kannan grinned. "Want to stay and watch me gut this beauty?"

They hastily declined—that fish was their travel companion. They would hate to see it skinned and sliced into neat slabs. They wished they could set it free, but it wouldn't be fair to Kannan and DoubleMean. Catching fish was their livelihood; they had to respect that.

The orange glow of the setting sun covered the sky like a circus tent. With Day One of their investigations almost over, Arj, Tam, and Mira got on their bikes and rode home, their heads filled with memories of the sea.

Sleuthing was fantastic fun.

SIX

THE ROOM NOBODY KNEW OF

The next day, the three of them woke up feeling exhausted. Spending a day on the water under a hot sun can do that.

Mira sighed. "If I were a fish, I'd have no energy to swim, and I'd drown."

"I am tired too," confessed Arj. "As Chief Detective, I declare today to be a day of rest."

To ensure the day wouldn't be a complete waste, he picked Mira to speak to Dumdumchechi. Tam and Arj weren't too keen to investigate her; she was a motormouth who wouldn't stop talking about her lost cows and her sad life.

Arj found an old phone in his dad's study and showed Mira how to record a conversation. "Before you step into the cowshed, press record. Like this. Give her about half an hour to talk, after which you can come back. Then Tam and I, Lieutenant Chief and Chief Detective, will listen closely to see if we can spot any holes in her story."

"Why should I do all the boring work?" protested Mira.

Tam snapped, "This is your training. If you don't want to do it, we can always find another Junior Detective."

Mira couldn't bear the thought of someone else taking her place. She agreed to go.

The cowshed was home to four cows—Gita, Rukmini, Laxmi, Parvati—and a bull, Shiva. Arj had tried to rename them Buttercup, Daisy, Penelope, Annabelle, and Samson. Dumdumchechi had laughed so much and pronounced their names so badly—"Budderkap, Dhaisee, Phenlow, Yannabhel, Shamsown"—he decided it was better to stick with the Indian names.

Mira could smell the strong odor of tobacco in the air long before she saw Dumdumchechi. As soon as Dumdumchechi saw Mira, she hastily stubbed out her beedi.

Mira wasn't fooled and looked at her reproachfully. "Smoking is bad for your health."

"I know, I know. I will quit next month. I swear on Rukmini."

Mira was skeptical. Everyone in the village knew Dumdumchechi swore on a cow for everything and never followed through on anything. Dumdumchechi quickly changed the topic and began complaining about how she had never had a vacation in her life.

The kids had heard many versions of her story. *You children have an easy life. I began working on my father's farm when I was six years old. My mother passed away when I was eight. I had to do all the housework. I had to get up at four in the morning, milk the cows, make breakfast, clean the house, and cook lunch. In the afternoon, I worked in the fields. After six o'clock, I would have to make dinner and clean up. By the time I could go to bed, I'd be dead tired.*

She looked at Mira wistfully. "I am sixty-six years old, and I have never had a day off. I wish I had my own cows."

Then, she began talking about her son. "Velu hasn't worked a single day in his life. It is my fault. I treated him like a prince. I sent him to the best schools. He didn't learn anything except how not to work. He has lived off his poor mother's earnings all his life."

"Did you know, Mira, I used to bring him to Lili Villa, hoping the doctors' positive influence would make him more responsible? He spent all his time lazing around. When he was sixteen, the police caught him stealing. I had to pawn my jewels to get him out. During those horrible days, my cows gave me comfort."

At this point, she grew a bit hysterical. "When Velu turned twenty-one, that son of a hippopotamus stole from me. He sold my cows on the cheap to our neighbor. You couldn't even get an old goat for that price. Who knows what he did with that money? I never saw a rupee of it. He disappeared after that day. I didn't even go looking for him. My heart has hardened—he is not my problem anymore."

Mira's attention wandered. She was listlessly staring at a wall when she suddenly realized Dumdumchechi had finished her story and was talking to someone on the phone. Mira tried to listen in, but she quickly hung up.

"I need to go—an emergency. I will continue my story some other time."

Mira was relieved and started to walk away. Suddenly, she stopped. A wonderful thought entered her head. *I could wait for Dumdumchechi to leave and investigate the cowshed all by myself. Tam and Arj will be so jealous. Serves them right for sending me here alone.*

Mira hid behind the big mango tree and watched Dumdumchechi amble away. Wisely, she didn't rush into the shed as soon as Dumdumchechi left. Mira counted to six hundred under her breath. At six hundred and one, she ran into the cowshed and looked around cautiously. There was no one there except for the cows placidly chewing cud. They looked so peaceful. She patted Parvati's soft forehead and whispered, "Do you know who the burglar is?"

She thought hard. Where would Dumdumchechi hide the gold if she had stolen it? Under the straw (not there), in the milk pail (no), in the water trough (nope), in a dark corner (empty), behind the thick collars the cows wore (just soft skin). She searched every inch of the cowshed but couldn't find anything. She squatted on the milk pail. As her eyes wandered around the room, she spotted a cloth hanging at the back of the cowshed. She had never noticed it before. It was red with yellow spots, and there were dark streaks of dirt on it. She wondered why someone would hang a cloth to dry in a musty cowshed. She walked up to the fabric and touched it. Her hand went right through the wall instead of hitting a hard surface.

Her mouth went dry. With trembling fingers, she pushed at the cloth again, and the edge lifted off the floor. It was a curtain covering a doorway!

Mira's mind was racing. *Should I run back and tell Tam and Arj about this discovery?* Mira wondered. *No! I will find things on my own and then report my findings to the Chief Detective and Lieutenant Chief. Hah! I might even get a promotion. I like the sound of Junior Chief Detective.*

She lifted the cloth off the nail and dropped it on the floor. As if by magic, the wall now had a hole. It opened into a small dark room with a wooden staircase at one end. She pulled out her phone and checked. "Phew! It has a flashlight. Goodbye, darkness." She turned it on, and its bright beam bounced off the walls. She began climbing the rickety wooden steps. When she placed her foot on the fourth step, a piece broke off and fell with a loud thud. Mira jumped, but she forced herself to give it another try.

She tried placing her other foot closer to the wall. The step seemed to hold. In this way, hugging the dusty wall, she climbed the staircase. After two flights of steps, she entered a room.

It was larger than the room downstairs, with windows on all four sides. Sunlight streamed in. Mira turned off the flashlight.

Someone was living here. There was a mat on the floor with a pillow at one end and a neatly folded bed sheet at the other. A little black stove sat in one corner. A rope was tied across the far end of the room with clothes hung out to dry. Mira recognized Dumdumchechi's unmistakable lungis and shirts.

She spotted a steel trunk in another corner. She opened it, almost expecting to find the stolen jewelry inside. Instead, she found more clothes, a photograph of cows, and a small bottle of perfume. The perfume bottle was empty. She also found a brown wallet. She forced herself to open it, knowing that her parents would disapprove.

"I am a Junior Detective. I am doing this to catch criminals," she whispered to herself. The wallet was empty too. She searched all the pockets; it had nothing, not even a coin. Feeling dejected, she shut the trunk and walked up to the stove. Bottles filled with oils and spices were neatly arranged around the stove.

That's when it hit Mira—*Dumdumchechi lives here! She doesn't have a house of her own. That's why she is always at Lili Villa, and no one has ever seen her arrive in the morning or leave in the evening.*

She felt sad for the old lady who had to live in this horrible room with so little. She was about to leave when she decided to look around the room one last time. She spotted something outside and almost fainted in excitement. A thick, strong-looking rope was tied to one of the window bars. It stretched from the cowshed to the roof of Lili Villa. Mira could see how convenient the rope would have been for the thief. Thombu had missed this vital clue because the cowshed was on the other side of the house.

Mira's brain was on fire. *If this rope is outside Dumdumchechi's window, she had to know the thief, right? I don't think Dumdumchechi could swing on the rope. She had to have a partner—a smaller, lighter, more agile partner.*

She quickly took a photograph of the rope stretching to the roof and then walked down the stairs carefully. She was dying to run home, but she was terrified of the wood giving way. When she reached the last step, she heaved a sigh of relief. She had gotten away without breaking any bones. Mira put the curtain back exactly as it was, using the milk pail as a step stool. She ran back to the house as fast as she could.

Tam and Arj had their noses buried in a comic. When Mira burst into the room, they looked up without much interest.

"Did one of the cows chase you?" Tam laughed at her dirt-streaked dress and red cheeks.

Mira ignored her question and began breathlessly telling them what she had discovered.

Arj's eyes widened. "I don't believe it. Let's go to the cowshed and see for ourselves."

The three of them ran to the shed and skidded to a stop at the entrance. Dumdumchechi was back; she was singing a song and milking Gita.

She looked up at the children and gave them a toothy smile. "How come I am so popular today? Everyone wants to see me."

The kids gave her a polite grin. They could see the curtain at the back in all its filthy brightness. They couldn't believe they had never spotted it before. They tried not to stare at it; they didn't want to make Dumdumchechi suspicious.

Dumdumchechi looked at them affectionately—a captive audience. She began where she'd left off.

"Lucky! You kids get to enjoy your summer vacation. You know, I have never had a single day off?"

They heard Pitamma call them for tea.

"Phoof!" murmured Tam. "Saved by food."

Tam and Arj dragged their feet back to Lili Villa, sorely disappointed they couldn't investigate the room upstairs. Mira skipped along beside them. She had had the best day ever.

"Being Junior Detective is amazing. Boring work can be a lot of fun!" Mira declared to a scowling Tam.

SEVEN

SHE WHIZZED AWAY IN A WHAT?

The neighbor's rooster crowed at six o'clock the following day. Unfortunately, the kids slept through the racket. They awoke two hours later in a panic, and they rushed to the cowshed without even brushing their teeth. They stopped short at the sight of Dumdumchechi's large back jiggling as she scrubbed Parvati with a stiff bristle brush.

They kept popping into the cowshed using the slightest of excuses.

"Pitamma needs some hay for the stove."

"Will you give me some cow pies for my dam?"

"Can I take a selfie with Shiva? He's so cute."

Dumdumchechi was flattered by all this attention. The kids had always avoided her, and to be showered with so much love now felt good. Unfortunately for the detectives, no matter how many times they dropped in, the cowshed was never free of her presence. She was always there, beaming at her unexpected visitors.

"Why can't she step out for half an hour?" grumbled Arj.

They sat around the dining table with glum faces when Tam had a brainwave. "Let's dip a handkerchief in some chloroform and cover Dumdumchechi's nose with it. One sniff and boom! She'll faint, and we can investigate in peace."

Arj glared at her. "Where do we find the chloroform, Miss Smarty Pants?"

Before the two of them could start arguing again, Mira quietly asked, "Why can't we investigate the rope from the outside?" Tam and Arj looked at Mira with newfound respect.

The detectives located the spot outside the cowshed and looked up. There was no rope connecting the cowshed to the main house. If it weren't for the photograph Mira had taken, no one would have believed her. Arj pulled out the phone and held up the image. It was a perfect match, except for the missing rope.

They were beginning to get a crick in their necks from staring at the roof when they heard Pitamma calling their names.

Arj raced to the kitchen, wondering what yumminess was in store for him. Instead, he found Taramma seated on a bench. Arj had never seen her look unhappy; she always appeared to glow with love and kindness.

Taramma held out a cloth bag for Arj. He thanked her and quickly opened it to find a box of coconut barfis and ginger candy. Arj gave her a hug and took off to share the goodies with the girls.

"Ginger candy is the best thing in the world," declared Tam. She had once tried to explain it to her friends back in school. "Imagine eating a piece of raw ginger with a mouthful of sugar, making your nose and eyes water. It's weird but really tasty."

Between bites, Mira whispered, "Amma said that Taramma shouldn't be spending her money on us."

Arj and Tam shifted uncomfortably. They could hear Sheila Ammayi's calm voice in their heads. *Taramma is a retired nurse who lives off a small pension. You cannot ask her for any treats; she needs that money to live.* They tried to explain to her that they never asked Taramma for anything and that Taramma was the one who always brought them presents. She never visited empty-handed; she was their Santa Claus in a white saree.

Tam dismissed the idea with her usual flippancy. "If Sheila Ammayi is uncomfortable, let her speak to Taramma. I think it'll sound insulting if we do it."

Arj and Mira nodded.

"Yes," agreed Mira. "Let Amma tell Taramma how to spend her money."

Having cleared that up, they felt less guilty about munching on the sweets when they heard Taramma yell, "Bye." The kids looked at each other, and the same thought flashed across their minds.

Arj, being Chief Detective, spoke up, "We could follow Taramma and see if we can figure out where she was on the night of the twelfth. She is a suspect, even if we like her."

They raced to get their bicycles to shadow Taramma. By the time they had unlocked and wheeled their bikes to the gate, Taramma was at some distance away, walking at a slow pace. The kids got off their bikes. If they pedaled, they would overtake Taramma in no time. Every good detective knows that they must keep the suspect in front of themselves, not behind.

Taramma turned the corner onto the main road and headed to the bus stop. They knew she always took a bus to Lili Villa because Taramma had a bus story every time she visited—how crowded it was, or whom she met, or how she taught a rude conductor some much-needed manners.

Arj hadn't thought this investigation through; it would have been impossible for them to have followed Taramma on a bus with their bikes. But they didn't have to.

Instead of crossing the road to get to the bus stop, Taramma opened the door of a black BMW and got in. Before they could say "fish fry", the car sped away, leaving three gaping detectives in the dust.

They were so focused on Taramma that they hadn't even noticed the car parked right in front of them.

Arj stroked his chin like a TV detective. "There is definitely something fishy going on here."

EIGHT

UP, DOWN, SIDEWAYS, AND ON YOUR HEAD

The detectives' heads were buzzing with theories about Taramma.

Tam had the most outlandish ones. "Taramma is a don—queen of all the thieves in Kerala. She probably gets her enemies killed and eats their eyeballs for breakfast."

"Seriously?"

Tam shrugged. "You never know."

Since no one was taking her seriously, she shot out a different suggestion. "Let's go to a movie. It will clear our heads."

Her cousins agreed. Their brains needed a rest.

There was only one theater in Elathoor, but it was a good one. During the summer, there was usually a kids' movie playing at three o'clock in the afternoon. Parents were happy when their children wanted to go to the movies because N. Master, a retired schoolteacher, ran the theater.

He sourced interesting films from all over the world, chosen because they were educational (the parents approved) and fun (the children approved) to watch. N. Master had good taste.

He was screening *The Wind Rises* by a Japanese filmmaker called Hayao Miyazaki that afternoon. It was about a boy who wanted to design airplanes, and by the end, Tam, Mira, and Arj decided they wanted to become aerospace engineers when they grew up. There was something about the movie that reminded them of the ocean.

Arj said, "It looked too real to be a cartoon."

After the film ended, Tam insisted that they thank N. Master. Arj and Mira tagged along, mumbling something about their "mad" cousin.

N. Master was pleasantly surprised. He beamed at them the entire time, his happiness bouncing around the room. Once they were outside his office, Tam remarked, "Everyone likes to be thanked, except animals, I guess. Animals don't care much for manners."

Suddenly, Mira pointed frantically at someone walking down the corridor.

Tam corrected her. "It is bad manners to point, and remember when you do, three fingers point back at you."

Arj shushed Tam. Mira had spotted Well-Cleaner Mani, one of their suspects!

They immediately decided to cancel their plans for the rest of the afternoon. Arj fished out a piece of paper and pencil from his pocket and scribbled a note: **Let's follow him. Don't talk. It will make him suspicious.**

Wow! thought Mira. *This feels so detective-ish.*

They tried to stay at a reasonable distance behind him. It had to be just right—not too far, or they would lose him, and not too close, or he would know he was being followed. It was quite tricky to do this as a team, and they kept bumping into each other. It didn't help one bit that Well-Cleaner Mani paused to look at every movie poster pasted on the theater walls.

Well-Cleaner Mani finally got on his bicycle, tested the bell—*tring-tring*—and whizzed away. The detectives scrambled to unlock their bikes, but they were soon on their way, pedaling furiously to keep up with him. He went through a green light at one point, and when the kids reached the signal, it turned red. They waited impatiently, wondering whether their suspect had slipped away for good. As soon as the light turned green, Arj pedaled with all his might. To his surprise, Well-Cleaner Mani hadn't gone far. He had stopped to buy cakes from a bakery.

"Dang!" muttered Arj. "I am hungry too, but the investigation comes first." He continued to tail Well-Cleaner Mani, turning to look wistfully at the many-colored cakes displayed in the bakery window.

After a whole heap of zigzagging, Well-Cleaner Mani stopped and wheeled his bicycle into a tiny cottage. It looked like it had popped out of a storybook—a green picket fence, white walls, a red roof, and a creeper with yellow-green flowers. The kids looked around.

"Where are we?" whispered Tam.

Arj shrugged. He had never been to this neighborhood before.

They didn't know what to do. Tam and Mira stared at the front door for a while. Arj idly wondered if he could send in a drone to monitor the suspect when Well-Cleaner Mani stepped out and excitedly waved at the kids. He had spotted them through the window.

"Oh, great!" said Tam sarcastically. "What kind of detectives are we if our suspect is so happy to see us?" They waved back reluctantly.

Arj called out, "We were biking around and seem to have lost our way."

Well-Cleaner Mani grinned. "I can help. I know all the roads in the village. Would you like a drink of water first?"

They nodded. Arj whispered, "Once inside the house, we can question him."

At the front step, the detectives paused, and three heads simultaneously tilted toward the ceiling. It was a strange place. Ropes hung from the roof, suspended four feet above the ground, with a large knot tied at the end.

Well-Cleaner Mani climbed up one of the ropes, his toes holding on to the knot. It was weird to see him standing high above the ground, swinging on the braided cord. Then he began performing some incredible moves. He turned upside down, twirled round and round, and leaped from rope to rope like Tarzan. He even let go of one rope midair, somersaulted, and, miraculously, before he could crash to the floor, managed to grab another rope gracefully.

There was something familiar about what he was doing. That's when it hit Arj. "It's a trapeze act! We've seen this before in the circus."

Well-Cleaner Mani finished with a double flip and landed in front of the children with a big grin on his face. He wasn't sweaty after all that hectic activity. Then, as if what he had done was the most ordinary thing in the world, he quietly walked to the back of the house and came back with three glasses of water. They sat cross-legged on the floor (there didn't seem to be any chairs or tables or sofas in that hall of ropes) and he told them his story.

"My mother is a Russian trapeze artist. She used to perform with the Bolshoi Circus. When they were touring India, the circus passed through Elathoor. Here, my mama met my papa, fell in love, and she decided to stay. Her real name is Ludmila, but all our neighbors call her Lila. She says this is the most beautiful village in the world."

They weren't sure if Well-Cleaner Mani was pulling their leg. They had seen his mother; she looked like a Malayali lady. She even had the famous Mallu curls. Her hair was a shade of brown, unlike the more common jet-black color, but they assumed it was because she never treated it with coconut oil.

Just then, Well-Cleaner Mani's mother walked in. Except she didn't exactly walk in.

Dressed in a mundu-veshti, she leaped into the house, caught a rope, and flew across the room. Two somersaults later, she landed at the door of the kitchen. That's when she noticed the children.

Well-Cleaner Mani explained why they were there. She smiled and asked in perfect Malayalam, "Would you like some pazhampori?"

The kids looked at Well-Cleaner Mani suspiciously. Was he telling them the truth? Yes, his house was weird, and they had witnessed this old lady turn somersaults in the air, but still. Well-Cleaner Mani sensed their disbelief. He walked into an inner bedroom and walked out with his birth certificate. It read:

This is to certify that
Vladislav Zakharov,
weighing 5 pounds 9 ounces,

was born on the 17th day of March in the year 2000
to Ludmila Zakharova and Sukumar Mani
in Saint Petersburg, Russia.

Well-Cleaner Mani (they couldn't pronounce Vladislav) added, a tad proudly, "I've got the original certificate in Russian, too."

Tam whispered, "There's no way anyone could have forged this."

Well-Cleaner Mani confided in them. "When I am old enough, I am going to Russia to join the Bolshoi Circus. That's why I practice eight hours a day, every day, training under my mother."

They could hear hot oil sizzling in the kitchen as Lila fried up a batch of bananas for pazhampori. Well-Cleaner Mani drew their attention to a framed piece of paper. It read (in both Russian and English):

The Acrobat Manifesto

Thou shalt not walk on the floor.
Thou shalt not weigh more than
one hundred and ten pounds.
Thou shalt not be scared of falling.
Thou shalt not stop practicing, even on Sundays.
Thou shalt not forget to catch thine partner midair.

The children were amazed. They couldn't believe Well-Cleaner Mani had such a colorful past and the potential to have such an exciting future. They looked at him with new respect.

Mira noticed the wall had small bumps on its surface.

"What are these for?"

"It's a climbing wall."

Well-Cleaner Mani showed them how to climb using the bumps. He taught them how to bend their fingers for better grip, how to place their toes in the grooves, and how to hoist their weight to move upwards. Before you knew it, the four of them were climbing the wall like monkeys.

When Lila walked in with the pazhampori, she couldn't find the children anywhere. She looked up, and sure enough, there they were, clinging to the ceiling. She hiked up her mundu, and, holding the plate with one hand, she climbed the wall and handed out the fried treats. The kids felt like chimps, eating above ground.

"This doesn't taste like Russian food. It's exactly like what Pitamma makes. Is your mum really Russian?" Mira asked.

Before Well-Cleaner Mani could answer, Tam dropped the plate with a clang. Luckily, all the banana fritters had been eaten up by then. They climbed down reluctantly. Being above ground was way better than being on it.

Well-Cleaner Mani didn't want them to go. He was eager for company and, because of his odd passion, he had no friends. Everyone thought he was nuts to choose climbing over football.

"Before you go, I have something to show you."

He dragged out a small wooden trunk labeled "My Treasures". He had scrawled the letters on the label with different-colored crayons.

He opened it to reveal a motley collection of objects—a rusty bell, a knife with a carved handle, a pearl, a bright orange starfish, a yellow baby rattle, an unidentifiable piece of metal, and a tiny pressure cooker, black all over and unusable.

"All collected from the bottom of wells I have dived into."

"Why would anybody throw a pressure cooker into a well? Is there a mystery to solve here?" Arj wondered aloud.

Tam made eyes at Mira and Arj, telepathically urging them to leave. Someone who collected junk could hardly be the burglar. She thought they were wasting their time here.

Well-Cleaner Mani noticed Tam's expression and knew his friends were about to say goodbye. To delay them, he rushed into another bedroom and pulled out a bunch of photographs.

The last thing the children wanted to see were hundreds of photos, but they remained seated. After all, he had taught them how to climb. The kids gazed at the pictures with polite disinterest. Tam paused at one picture. It was a shot of Well-Cleaner Mani holding up something underwater. She showed it to Arj.

Well-Cleaner Mani explained, "This was taken by a National Geographic photographer. He was filming a rare type of plant in the seabed near Elathoor when his wedding ring fell into the water. He tried looking for it but couldn't find it. Someone from his team told him about me and how good I am at finding things stolen by the sea. The water was dark and cold, but I was fearless. The foreigner was wearing an oxygen cylinder, a mask, and a diving costume, while I only had a pair of swimming trunks. I found the ring on the first dive. The photographer took this with his underwater camera. I smiled for him, and the water hit my teeth and tasted weird. I then swam upwards and broke the surface, holding up the ring. Everyone clapped," boasted Well-Cleaner Mani.

Arj fervently hoped Tam wouldn't show interest in another photograph. Well-Cleaner Mani was full of himself and, given the slightest encouragement, he would talk about his achievements for a week. This time, Arj tried to signal Tam that it was time they left.

Unfortunately, Tam wasn't looking at him. She was still staring at the photo. Not to be left out, Mira peered at it too.

Poor Well-Cleaner Mani was a bit confused. He was hoping they would move on to the next photo so that he could entertain them with another story. He decided to get a glass of water and walked into the kitchen. As soon as he left, Tam urgently pointed to the right-hand corner of the photo. Arj and Mira finally saw what she was so excited about. The date and time were clearly printed: 05/12, 01:12.

Well-Cleaner Mani returned with another box. The children hastily stood up.

"We have to get back, or our parents will worry."

Just as they were leaving, Well-Cleaner Mani lowered his voice and whispered, "You know, I think Kodavis is the one who burgled your house. The night of the burglary, at around 1:45 a.m., I was on my way home with the photographer when the two of us saw Kodavis sneaking out of the gate at Lili Villa. What was he doing at your house at that time of night?"

Tam blurted, "This is proof! We have a witness now. It has to be Kodavis!"

They thanked Well-Cleaner Mani for the information and hurried home, bursting with excitement. At the gate, Tam and Arj got into a huge argument. Arj wanted to tell Thombu immediately. Tam said they should wait until they were sure and only then present it to Thombu.

"If we accuse Kodavis and it turns out to be not true, then we won't be able to use his bike. That will be the end of our detective work," Tam reasoned. "Worse than that, Sheila Ammayi will find out and may even ban us from going out on our own."

Mira sided with Tam. She knew if Kodavis's bicycle were out of the picture, Tam would take hers, and she would be left behind. Arj finally gave in and agreed with the girls.

That night, the three of them could hardly sleep. They couldn't figure how to investigate Kodavis, their prime suspect.

Arj said, "How do we follow him when he is with Amma-Appa all day? I'm almost certain he is the thief."

Tam and Mira agreed. They hated Pinchy-Fingers Kodavis. It would be so satisfying to see him behind bars, unable to pinch anyone ever again.

NINE

THE ART OF THE MATTER

There were two strong suspects now—retired nurse Taramma, who drove around in luxury cars, and Kodavis, the driver, who snooped around the house at night.

"I think it will be easier to investigate Taramma first," said Arj. "Let's ask Amma for her address. We can head over there tomorrow and see what we can find."

With the confidence of having been a successful Junior Detective, Mira piped up, "Amma will want to know why we need her address."

Arj was waiting to be asked. He pounced on Mira. "Good question, Junior Detective! We'll tell her we want to send Taramma a thank-you card for all the goodies she brings us. Since you asked the question, you get to design the card." Tam and Arj sniggered, but Mira didn't mind. She loved coloring and making art.

After a breakfast of dosas and fiery red-onion chutney the next morning, Arj asked his mother for Taramma's mailing address. Sheila Ammayi was most pleased to give it when they told her why they wanted it. Mira held out the card on cue.

"This card will make her so happy," exclaimed Sheila Ammayi.

Mira's card was beautiful, shaped like a present with ribbons. She had written a little thank-you poem inside:

Dear Taramma,

You make us happy,

When days are yucky.

Your gifts are thoughtful.

You are wonderful.

We thank you for your kindness.

We wish you lots of happiness.

Love,

Mira, Tam, Arj

Everyone around the table appreciated Mira's creativity.

And, now they had Taramma's home address. Arj looked at it. "It's not too far from here. Maybe a thirty-minute ride."

After their parents left, Pitamma handed them a bag filled with snacks.

"Does she read minds? How did she know we were going to look for Taramma's house?" Mira wondered.

It was a lovely day for a bike ride. They reached the neighborhood of Nadakkavu, which is where Taramma lived, and looked for Sixth Street. They found it easily enough and rode down the lane, searching for Number 874.

The street was lined with small houses, their facades unpainted, and their front yards overgrown with weeds. The kids felt a bit sad to think that Taramma lived here and chose to spend what little money she had on them. When they finally found her house, they discovered a crumbling little cottage with half a roof.

"I don't think anyone lives here," said Tam.

They were debating whether to push the rusty gate open when an old man walked past them.

"Hello, uncle!" Arj immediately called out to him. "Does retired nurse Taramma live here?"

He flashed a toothless smile. "She used to, but that lucky woman now lives in a big house in White Gardens."

"Is White Gardens far from here?"

"No, it's just ten minutes away. And you are. . .?"

The minute they told him they were Dr. Damodar's family, he became extra helpful. He gave them Taramma's new address and mapped out the easiest route to get there.

They thanked him, and as they were cycling away, he yelled, "Tell your father that Chickenpox Balan sends his regards!"

The directions were precise; the detectives reached White Gardens in under ten minutes. The difference between the two neighborhoods was startling. Here, the houses were huge, much bigger than Lili Villa. They had lush lawns, high boundary walls, and Arj spotted different brands of luxury cars parked in the driveways. He almost forgot why he was there, he was so busy admiring the fancy cars.

When they found Number 22, the three of them gazed at it in awe. It was a towering palace with a roof studded with blue tiles.

"It looks like those mansions we see on TV," Mira whispered.

The kids wheeled their bikes up to the large black gate and rang the bell. A small window dropped open with a clang.

A guard poked his head out. "What are you doing here?"

"We. . . we'd like to see Taramma," Arj stammered, wondering if Tam was right after all. *Is Taramma the queen of thieves? Will we get into trouble for coming over here?*

The window banged shut, leaving the three of them feeling very small.

After what seemed like ages, the gate slid open, revealing a pretty pathway leading up to the house.

"Park your bikes next to the steel-gray Jaguar and walk up to the front door. Be careful. Don't scratch the car," the guard instructed them in a sharp voice. They did so without a word, feeling a bit intimidated.

They passed a swimming pool to the left, and the black BMW they had seen earlier was parked in the open garage on the right. After a long walk, the trio finally reached the front door. They were about to ring the bell when the door was thrown open, and Taramma welcomed them with a happy grin. She hugged them in turn, and they felt some of their fear melt away.

She rushed them in like a kid at a birthday party. "How did you find me? You should have called. I would have come over to your house."

Taramma's house had fancy decor—plush carpets, floor-to-ceiling curtains, white-and-gold sofas, and heavy wood furniture everywhere. Tam, Arj, and Mira followed her to the TV room, which was larger than most rooms in Lili Villa. A gigantic TV covered an entire wall. Facing the screen was a leather sofa that could seat at least twelve people. Taramma got them all to sit down and pressed a blue button. Within a few minutes, a man entered the room, dressed in a white outfit and a red turban.

She asked them if they wanted something to eat and placed an order for unnakkai, cookies, cakes, and juice.

The detectives stared at Taramma, unsure of what to say. She smiled, noticing their confusion, and gently asked again, "What brings you here, my children?"

Mira shyly held out the card. Taramma read it carefully, her eyes filling with tears.

Soon after, the turbaned man brought them a platter of snacks and, as they tucked in, Taramma began to tell them her story.

"Have you met Mohan, my son? Even as a child, he could draw very well. I don't know where he got his talent; no one else in the family can even draw a stick figure. When he turned sixteen, he began selling his canvases to tourists. A French traveler was impressed by his talent and offered him a scholarship to study art in Paris. Now he holds solo exhibitions in New York, London, Rome, Berlin. . . all over the world. He tells me he is very famous and that there is great demand for his work. This house is a gift from him."

Taramma wistfully looked around the room. "Some days, I miss the simple life I used to have. . . I don't even know where my son is in this big house."

Seeing that they had finished eating, she offered to show them around the house. On the first floor, they walked into a room to find a large man sprawled on a beanbag in front of an empty canvas.

It was Mohan, Taramma's son. He came up to them and effortlessly picked his mother up.

"Are these three your Lili Villa children?"

She squirmed and nodded. Mohan gently placed her down and gave her a loud kiss on the cheek. She giggled like a little girl.

He walked up to Arj and stared at him. Then, he held Arj's chin in his hands and turned his face from side to side. Arj looked back defiantly. No one could outstare him, except perhaps Damodar Ammavan.

Finally, Mohan asked Arj, "Will you pose for me? I want to paint you.

"What! Yes, of course!" Arj puffed up with pride.

With Arj posing for Mohan, Mira and Tam settled in to watch a French movie, *The Triplets of Belleville,* on Taramma's giant TV screen. Toward the end, Tam declared, "I don't think I can bear to watch anything on our little TV ever again."

The girls went to check on Arj. They found him sprawled on the beanbag, reading a comic. Tam and Mira sneaked up to peek at Arj's portrait. It looked a little like this: *Three circles. One large red circle and two small ones. One of the smaller circles is black with a neat brown handle. The second circle is brown with a black dot inside it.*

Apparently, this was postmodernist Arj. The large red

circle was Arj, the smaller black circle was a magnifying glass with a wooden handle, and the third circle was his eye.

"Oh well, whatever." Tam shrugged. "I don't get it, but it's cool to think this painting will be traveling to New York and hanging on the wall of a museum."

"Why is there a magnifying glass in the painting?" Mira asked. She hoped Arj hadn't blabbed to Mohan and given away their real reason for being here.

Mohan looked at her, puzzled. "You don't know? Arj wants to be a detective when he grows up."

"I do too!" yelled Tam.

"Me too," squeaked Mira.

Mohan smiled at the three excited faces. "Well, then I hope you come across a mystery to solve."

Hah! If only he knew, thought Arj. They said their goodbyes to Mohan.

At the front door, Taramma said, "The good doctors don't know about Mohan's good fortune. I want to live a simple village life. If you can, please don't tell anyone about this house." The kids nodded and hugged her. Her secret was safe with them.

On their way home, Arj crossed her off the list of suspects. "It can't be Taramma. She is so rich; she wouldn't need to steal from other people."

Tam, as usual, tried to poke a hole in his theory. "What if she is a kleptomaniac?"

Mira looked confused. It was a word she had never heard before.

"A kleptomaniac is someone who needs to take things that don't belong to them," Tam explained. "You have to nick something, no matter how much money you already have. The only way to cure it is to see a doctor. A girl in our class was caught stealing erasers, but they didn't punish her. Our science teacher explained the illness and made us promise we would never call her a thief."

Arj disagreed. "If Taramma had a medical problem, our mother would know. I am sure Taramma is innocent."

"I am so glad," cried Mira. "Of all our suspects, I like her best!"

TEN

AN ARREST IS MADE
AND SO IS AN ENEMY

Arj, Tam, and Mira spent the morning marveling at the fact that everyone they had investigated so far had a secret. Well-Cleaner Mani was half-Russian, their beloved Taramma was wealthy, DoubleMean was friendly to cats, and Dumdumchechi lived above the cowshed.

Mira sighed. "These are people we meet all the time. You wouldn't suspect they had anything to hide, and yet. . ."

"Everyone has a secret," Tam claimed.

"Really?" challenged Arj. "What's yours?"

Tam looked thoughtful. "I'll tell you mine if you both promise to tell me something you haven't told anyone before." Arj and Mira nodded.

Tam went first. "When I am in trouble, I pray to my father. I feel he watches over me and protects me from harm." She paused and took a deep breath. Arj and Mira felt sorry for Tam. They didn't realize she spoke to her father even though she had been too young to have known him before he died. Arj pulled out a bunch of books hidden inside his desk. They were thick and appeared well used. They were bound practice test papers for the All-India Medical Entrance Test. "I don't want to be a detective when I grow up. I want to be a doctor like Appa and Amma. I thought if I begin studying for it now, I surely will get into medical school." Tam and Mira could see how much this meant to him.

They looked at little Mira, wondering what her secret could be. Much to their surprise, she began bawling. Between sobs, she said, "There is this horrible, mean, spiteful girl at school who bullies me. She is taller than me and has huge nostrils. She takes my pocket money, and she makes me do her homework. The worst part is when she snaps her fingers and yells, 'Bag girl!' I have to carry her schoolbag."

"I haven't told anyone. If I complain to the teacher, I'll become unpopular, a snitch, and nobody will ever want to be my friend. She is the class monitor, and everyone listens to her. She chooses a new person to bully every year, but this time, she said I was such a good bag girl, she is keeping me on for one more year." Mira began to cry again. "I can't go through one more term of carrying that horrid girl's bag."

Tam wished she could punch that girl. *Only Arj and I have the right to boss Mira around,* she thought fiercely and put her arm around Mira's shoulder.

"How dare she? I promise before my summer vacation ends, I am going to take care of this girl."

Mira felt better. If Tam said she would do something, she would do it. She had little respect for bullies or rules. This girl was going to get the shock of her life.

Damodar Ammavan's shouting brought them back to the present. He was in the dining room with Thombu. He sounded furious.

"I don't believe it's him. I have met him, and he seems like a decent fellow. Where is the proof of his guilt?"

Thombu noticed the kids watching him and tried to get them on his side. He announced with pride, "I have arrested the thief, Well-Cleaner Mani. In fact, that is not even his real name." He looked around, expecting them to be surprised. Instead, the kids giggled.

Thombu ignored their strange reaction and continued. "His real name is Vlad-something. A Russian name. Yes, he is Russian; his mother is a trapeze artist posing as a Malayali aunty all these years. She must have been the one who climbed the walls at Lili Villa. Can a regular person do that, tell me? Nobody can hide the truth from Thombu for too long. I discovered this through a difficult and dangerous investigation. If they had known what I was up to, they might have tried to silence me." At this point, Tam burst out laughing. He sounded so dramatic. The cousins knew how sweet Well-Cleaner Mani and his mother were.

Thombu went purple in the face. "How dare you laugh at me? Don't you know I am a sub-inspector?"

Damodar Ammavan was curious, his bushy eyebrows framed like question marks. Tam, Arj, and Mira explained how Well-Cleaner Mani had invited them to his house and how they had found a photograph that gave him an alibi.

Damodar Ammavan looked stern. "Where is Well-Cleaner Mani now?"

Thombu glared at the children. "He's locked up at the police station. How do you explain this then: a large sum of money was deposited in the mother's account on the 13th of May, a day after the robbery. Trust me, Damu. It is Mani and his mother, Lila. I know the criminal type."

"I hope for your sake you haven't made a mistake, Thombu. Let's go to the police station and speak to Well-Cleaner Mani."

The children pleaded with Damodar Ammavan to take them along. They had never been to a police station before.

There, their friend was locked up in a cell. Mira walked up to him and held his hands through the bars. He was sobbing so much that he couldn't speak. Arj and Tam looked around. The police station didn't seem so frightening. It was just a large hall with three cells. In place of doors, the cells were guarded by long iron bars that ran from the roof to the floor.

Tam thought they looked like bird cages made of concrete and steel. A large wooden desk stood in the middle of the hall with a nameplate that read "Thombu T. Illayath, Sub-Inspector".

Three fierce-looking men played a game of cards in the second cell. The third cell held the largest man they had ever seen. He was almost seven feet tall. Tam stared at him open-mouthed when he looked straight at her and winked. Then, he grinned, revealing a mouth full of golden teeth. Suddenly afraid, Tam held Arj's hand. He was quite surprised, for Tam rarely showed any affection toward him.

Damodar Ammavan didn't seem to notice the other criminals. He spoke firmly to Thombu, "Release the boy. I will accept all responsibility for him." Damodar Ammavan was the only person who could talk to Thombu like that. Thombu agreed, and all of them got into the police jeep and drove to Well-Cleaner Mani's house.

Luckily, Mani's mother didn't know anything about the arrest. She was swinging from the ropes when they arrived. She jumped down in a hurry when she saw her son with the village doctor and his kids, accompanied by the pompous sub-inspector. She knew there was trouble brewing. As soon as the situation was explained to her, she began yelling at the top of her voice. Thankfully, all the words were in Russian, and no one could understand the insults.

When she finally calmed down, Mira gently asked her to bring out the box of photographs.

Thombu sulked in a corner while the rest of the group thumbed through the pictures. Finally, Mira found it—Well-Cleaner Mani underwater, triumphantly holding up a ring and grinning at the camera. The time and date were still clearly visible in the corner.

Mira took it to Thombu, who snorted. "With today's technology, anyone can change the date."

"If you don't trust the photo, why don't you check with the person who took it? Surely a reputed National Geographic photographer wouldn't lie?" said Damodar Ammavan.

Thombu muttered something under his breath. It was just as well that no one heard him. Then, he suddenly remembered. "How come you made such a large deposit of cash into your account on the 13th of May?" He sneered. "Isn't it money from the sale of stolen jewelry?"

Well-Cleaner Mani's mother glared at Thombu before marching into one of the rooms. Tam wondered, *Is she going to come out with a knife or a rifle? Or one of those hanging ropes? She could easily strangle Thombu with that.*

She returned instead with a piece of paper and thrust it in Thombu's face. "This is a copy of the bill we gave the photographer. He was so grateful to get his wedding ring back that he paid us extra. That was the money in the account. Any other questions?"

Thombu scowled. "I will check everything out, and if your answers don't add up, I will be back." He left in a huff. Damodar Ammavan apologized to Well-Cleaner Mani and his mother, and the kids gave their friend a big hug.

Back in the jeep, Damodar Ammavan gently advised Thombu, "You have to be careful. Incidents like this can cost you your job."

Thombu kept quiet and stared at the road. At a red light, he turned around and glared at the children in the back seat. "Don't think that you are very clever. You just got lucky this time."

As soon as Thombu turned his back, the trio giggled and silently high-fived each other. They felt like the best detectives in the world at that moment.

ELEVEN

A PHONE CALL IS OVERHEARD
AND A TRAP IS SET

Thombu marched into Lili Villa at around eight o'clock the following day. "I need to investigate Pitamma. I have waited long enough."

Damodar Ammavan sighed and reluctantly asked her to join them in the dining room. Pitamma emerged from the kitchen with a rolling pin in one hand. She was in the middle of rolling out perfect circles of dough to make puris for breakfast. Thombu stepped back a little. She was two inches taller than him and looked threatening.

Thombu stammered, "I. . . I. . . I need to ask you. . . s-s-some questions."

"Ask," growled Pitamma. Tam and Mira couldn't stop sniggering.

"What were you doing on the night of the burglary? I need details," Thombu demanded.

She pointedly looked at him. "Sleeping after an honest day's labor, unlike some people."

Thombu bristled. "What do you mean by that? Are you saying I am not honest?"

Sheila Ammayi intervened. "We have to get to work. Cooperate with Thombu, Pitamma. Please."

Three hours later, the doctors were home for lunch, only to find nothing to eat. Pitamma was seated in the kitchen, calmly reading a newspaper. She shrugged. "I can't cook. Your Thombu has taken over the kitchen. He is looking for gold and diamonds in the flour and rice bins."

They found Thombu in the pantry, squatting on the floor and going through every box, bin, and jar. His usually crisp uniform was dusted with flour, and his face was beet red. He was sweating profusely.

Damodar Ammavan tried not to laugh. He left his old friend to his investigations and took the family out for biryani and ice cream. The owner of the restaurant, Diarrhea Dineshan, was one of Damodar Ammavan's ex-patients; he refused to take any money from the good doctor. He even handed them two boxes of mutton biryani for Thombu and Pitamma as they were leaving.

At home, the family found a glum Thombu seated in a corner while Pitamma was cheerfully singing an old Malayalam song off-key. She spotted them and hooted, "Mr. Suspicious didn't find anything! Shall we go to his house and ransack his kitchen? After all, his footprint was a perfect fit, too!"

Thombu picked up his box of biryani and quietly slipped away. That night, and for two days after that, food from Pitamma's kitchen was burned, undercooked, over-salted, and generally terrible. Damodar Ammavan and Sheila Ammayi decided to leave Pitamma alone and not say a word about the food.

On the morning of the third day, Pitamma served beautiful, fluffy appams and a delicious vegetable stew as if by magic. The kids had lain low while Pitamma stewed and stormed. The tension at home was unbearable, but now that Pitamma was back to her usual self, they wondered whom they should investigate next. While they were making up their minds, Arj happened to overhear a *very* interesting conversation.

After breakfast, Arj was working on his dam when he needed some more mud. He walked toward the garage to fetch a spade when he froze in his tracks. He could hear Kodavis talking to someone in an urgent voice.

"I can't get you any more stuff. They are suspicious around here after the burglary." Pause. "Yes, I know I promised two more deliveries." Pause. "I can't return the money. . . I spent it." Pause. "Okay, let me see what I can do. I will try again tonight." Pause. "Yes, I know what will happen to me if I don't deliver."

Arj's heart was pounding, and his mind was racing. *What is Kodavis up to? What does he have to deliver? Is this connected to the burglary? Is he the thief?*

He didn't want Kodavis to realize that he had listened in on his conversation. He began whistling and pretended to walk toward the garage entrance. When he walked in, he noticed Kodavis was looking a little rattled. He was staring at his phone and didn't even acknowledge Arj's presence. He picked up the spade and walked out, still whistling. Once he was far from the garage, he raced to tell the girls. The detectives were excited. It would be perfect if Kodavis turned out to be the thief.

Tam suggested they should stay awake to see what Kodavis was up to. They decide to take turns.

10:00 p.m. to 12:00 a.m.—Mira takes the first watch
12:01 a.m. to 3:00 a.m.—Arj stays awake
3:01 a.m. to 6:00 a.m.—Tam plays watchman

They didn't think Kodavis would do anything after six o'clock because the sun would be up by then. In the evening, Arj and Tam sent Mira to ask Pitamma for some snacks. She came back loaded with chips, biscuits, a big bunch of grapes, and a flask of Bournvita.

"She didn't ask why! She didn't even say something boring like eating at night would spoil our appetite at breakfast. She is pure awesomesauce."

That night, the detectives were buzzing with nervous energy. They couldn't sleep; all of them stayed awake through Mira's watch. She protested, "I wanted to do this alone. You both are spoiling my fun."

At midnight, Arj asked Mira and Tam to get some rest. Mira crashed without protesting. Tam tried to stay awake, but within half an hour, she was in snoozeland, too.

Arj listened to the girls breathing peacefully beside him for a while. He thought about everyone fast asleep at Lili Villa—Amma and Appa in their bedroom, Pitamma in the room above the storeroom, Dumdumchechi above the cows, and Whisko curled up at the foot of their bed. Everyone was dreaming, except for him. . . and Kodavis.

He took a sip of Bournvita and looked out of the window. Nothing seemed to be amiss, but he couldn't shake the feeling that something or someone was in the yard.

He poked Tam, who shot up and looked around in alarm. She was only half asleep. Mira, on the other hand, was sleeping peacefully, dreaming many wonderful dreams. Arj nodded at Tam. She understood. *Don't wake Mira up.* They gingerly slid off the bed and slipped into their shoes. Arj picked up a hockey stick, and Tam gripped a cricket bat for protection. They tiptoed into the backyard.

At first, they couldn't see anything. Then, Arj nudged Tam. In the distance, they could see a dark figure outside their parents' consulting room. Tam was about to approach the figure when Arj shook his head.

They made their way back to the house. Once they were inside, they crept to the consulting room. They could see Kodavis clearly through a window from there. He was outside, peering into the disposal bin for expired medicines. It was a big white trash can, operated with a foot pedal; the doctors used it to dump empty medicine boxes. The kids had been warned never to go near the bin and, on no account, to touch any of the contents. Every Sunday, a big van would collect the trash and drive away.

Kodavis was rummaging through the trash, his gloved hand dipping in to pick up cartons and drop them into a large sack. They watched him for a while, unable to understand his actions. At one point, he looked straight at them. Tam felt a cough coming, but she held her silence.

After what felt like a long time, Kodavis stopped. He looked around and quickly walked away.

Arj and Tam weren't sure what to do. They went back to their room, wondering whether they should wake Damodar Ammavan up, but it might be ridiculous. Kodavis could be picking up cardboard for recycling. They decided to sleep on it.

When Arj opened his eyes the following morning, Mira was hovering over him impatiently. "Tell me! Tell me! What happened?"

Arj was too groggy to remember. Mira thought it was safe to shake Tam awake. Tam almost jumped out of bed. That's when Arj and Tam remembered what they had seen. They quickly filled Mira in.

They rushed outside and made a beeline for the disposal bin. The kids walked up to it, nervously keeping an eye out for the doctors, and pressed the foot pedal. Inside, they could see empty cardboard boxes of expired medicines in every color. Mira spotted an empty vitamin bottle that used to contain the yucky tablets they were forced to take every day. Mixed in were a few dirty-looking rolls of cotton gauze.

Mira ran her shoe over the dirt, creating a furrow. "It doesn't make sense. Why is Kodavis picking up empty medicine cartons? Why would he go through rubbish?"

That morning, Pitamma served them hot golden-brown vadas with green chutney. Damodar Ammavan happily tucked into them; it was one of his favorite breakfasts. The kids impatiently waited for him to finish, after which Arj asked as casually as he could, "Appa, are empty medicine cartons of any use?"

Damodar Ammavan looked up in a panic. He scoffed, "Of course not!" Then he went on to give them a lecture.

"I hope you kids haven't handled any expired medicines. They are dangerous. These drugs lose their strength after the expiration date. If a patient takes it when he is sick, he will not get better. That's not all. Sometimes, the chemicals in the medicines change over time and become poisonous. Or, if the medicine is a liquid, harmful bacteria can grow in it. Imagine putting bacteria-filled eye drops into your eyes. You could seriously damage your vision, even go blind."

Arj, Mira, and Tam hadn't realized that expired medicines could be so lethal. They would never use them in their lives.

Arj, being a good detective, patiently repeated his question, "Not the medicines, the cartons. Could they be useful?"

Damodar Ammavan's eyebrows rose a fraction. "Why? Cartons are just paper but don't you dare touch them. Some of the medicines may have leaked onto the cardboard, and they could be poisonous."

After Damodar Ammavan left for work, they began discussing Kodavis's motives.

"Why was he collecting the cartons, which are not only useless but could be dangerous?" They couldn't think of a single reason for Kodavis's behavior.

"I think we should let Appa question Kodavis," Mira suggested.

Arj shook his head. "He will probably deny the whole thing. He could easily say he dropped something precious like a ring or a phone in the bin and pretend to have been looking for it. No, we need to figure out a way to catch him red-handed. I am sure he will return. I clearly heard him say he had to make two deliveries."

"Let's stay awake every night until Kodavis comes back," said Tam excitedly. She loved these midnight adventures.

Arj's eyes lit up. He moved in closer and whispered a plan.

Tam grinned. "Yes, it could work. We can set it up at half past eight in the evening after Kodavis leaves, and we can take it down before he returns in the morning."

That evening, Kodavis left for home at the usual time. After dinner, everyone at Lili Villa retreated to their bedrooms. Once the lights were switched off around ten o'clock, Tam, Arj, and Mira silently made their way to the disposal bin.

A straight path ran through the yard from the doctors' consulting room to Lili Villa's outer gates. Lining the pathway were coconut trees. Arj tied a rope from a coconut tree to the bars of the consulting room's window. It was loose and lay flat on the ground so that when Kodavis came toward the bins, he wouldn't notice it.

After tying the rope, the trio went inside to wait in the consulting room, sipping Bournvita in tiny mouthfuls to pass the time. They didn't want to take turns—all three wanted to be a part of this adventure, and none of them could bear the thought of sleeping.

"Don't get too excited. Kodavis may not come back tonight," Arj warned.

At around half past one, they heard footsteps outside the room. They looked out.

It was a full moon. Tam whispered, "Isn't he stupid to come out tonight when there is a giant flashlight in the sky?"

"I think he is frightened and probably wants to get the job done quickly," said Arj.

Kodavis began picking up the medicine cartons again. Tam and Mira carefully pulled the rope taut to stretch across the path, two feet above the ground. They tied their end of the rope to Damodar Ammavan's heavy desk for safety. Arj sneaked up behind Kodavis with a hockey stick as Tam and Mira watched from the window and gave the signal.

"Police!"

Kodavis sprung up like he had been bitten by a snake and ran toward the gate. He was going so fast that he didn't notice the rope. He tripped and took a nasty fall, rolling on the ground a few times. Arj blocked his path to stop him in case he tried to run again, but there was no need. Kodavis was holding his leg and yelping in pain.

The lights came on in Damodar Ammavan and Sheila Ammayi's room. Tam and Mira quickly untied the rope so that it fell back to the ground. Arj threw the hockey stick away. He had a feeling his father wouldn't approve.

Damodar Ammavan walked out to find Kodavis on the ground, bawling like a baby. He was still clutching the bag of empty medicine cartons. Pitamma came on the scene, armed with a sickle. "If you are here to steal something, you have to get past me first." She looked frightening.

Damodar Ammavan looked grim. "Keep an eye on him. Make sure he doesn't run away."

Arj helped Kodavis stand up and, along with his father, helped him limp into the consulting room.

The doctor examined his leg. Kodavis's ankle was swollen. "I don't think anything is broken. It is a sprain, not a fracture. You probably twisted your foot in the fall. Take these painkillers three times a day for three days, and you will be fine."

Once Kodavis realized that he hadn't broken his leg, he began to feel *very* afraid.

"Now," continued Damodar Ammavan, "tell me what you were doing outside my house at this time of night." Everyone eyed Kodavis with suspicion. He didn't respond. Damodar Ammavan pulled out his phone and began to make a call to his friend Thombu.

Kodavis started sobbing again. "I was only taking what nobody wanted, what you throw away. It's not really stealing."

Slowly the whole horrific story poured out. "I supply these cartons to a contact who then sells them to a gang. This gang manufactures sugar pills that look like medicine tablets. They insert the sugar pills into empty cartons, passing them off as genuine medication. They sell these to people living in the forests of Wayanad. These people can't read or write, but they recognize the cartons, so they trust the seller. There are no clinics, doctors, or nurses in this remote area. Most of them are happy to get any kind of medicine, and my contact sells them cheaply. It doesn't harm them. It may even help them get better. Doctor, you have said so many times yourself—believing you can get better is half the battle. You could call what I am doing a form of social work."

Damodar Ammavan exploded. "You wicked man! How dare you exploit those innocent people? Fake medicines can kill them. I blame myself—Sheila and I are responsible for not disposing of our medicine cartons correctly. I don't want to see you again. Get out of my house."

After Kodavis limped out, everyone went back to their rooms. They couldn't believe someone could be so rotten as to cheat innocent people.

Arj and Tam sneaked up to the consulting room very early the following morning and undid the rope. They returned it to the garage. The kids couldn't help feeling thrilled, but they didn't dare show it.

Damodar Ammavan and Sheila Ammayi stayed home that day and called a professional company to dispose of the empty cartons.

A large gray van rolled into Lili Villa's driveway. Three men, wearing masks and gloves, gathered all the waste into three large bags. These bags would then be fed into a giant machine, which would crush the innocent-looking-but-dangerous boxes into pulp. They also placed a proper disposal machine outside the clinic. It had a slot like a mailbox (but much bigger). Cartons could be dropped through the opening, and they would be automatically shredded. Damodar Ammavan also asked the men to take the old bin away. He never wanted to see it again.

The kids were glad that they didn't have to deal with Pinching Kodavis anymore. The only thing they would miss was his bike. Arj, in a fit of generosity, said, "I can take Mira on my bike, and Tam can ride Mira's."

The detectives had solved one mystery, but the burglary remained unsolved. The only people left on their list of suspects were Veer Sagar, Fan-Fixer Faekku, and Dumdumchechi. It had to be one of them or, as Tam imagined, *It could be all three of them.*

TWELVE

THE SECOND-TO-LAST SUSPECT

Lunch had just ended at Lili Villa. The grown-ups were planning on settling in for an afternoon siesta when Thombu walked in, twirling his gold-rimmed sunglasses. He seemed particularly pleased with himself and hollered for a glass of water. When it was brought out to him, he noticed the rim of the glass was dirty. Pitamma still hadn't forgiven him.

He put the glass down and began bragging about how brave he had been. "While all of you were asleep last night, we received an anonymous tip about a gang of smugglers operating in the forest. I set off with another constable without waiting for reinforcements. I wasn't scared, of course. I had a job to do." He then gave a slightly exaggerated account of an arrest, which included him leaping from tree to tree. "Those rascals were selling fake medicines to the people who live in the forest. We caught four members of the gang and sent them to New Delhi for questioning. My boss is incredibly pleased; he even hinted at a promotion.

Damu, I now need to solve your case to become inspector."

After Thombu left, Sheila Ammayi confessed, "I called the station. I couldn't bear to let those criminals go unpunished."

Damodar Ammavan nodded. "That was smart. I was feeling guilty about not reporting them."

That evening, tucking into a bowl of bilimbis coated with salt, the detectives pored over the list of suspects, making notes. It didn't look good.

1) Pitamma: Couldn't find gold in the pantry. Most likely innocent.

2) Dumdumchechi: Why was the rope tied from her window to the roof of the house?

3) Kodavis: Found guilty of another crime.

4) DoubleMean: On a boat in the middle of the ocean the night of the burglary

5) Fan-Fixer Faekku: To be investigated.

6) Well-Cleaner Mani: Has an alibi—a photograph that proves his innocence.

7) Taramma: Can buy all the gold she wants. She doesn't have to steal from the doctors.

8) Veer Sagar: To be investigated.

Next on the list was Fan-Fixer Faekku. They didn't know much about him. He was a short, skinny man. He spoke with a stammer that would make an appearance only when he talked about money.

Tam had an idea. She dug out a screwdriver and handed it to Arj.

"Why don't you mess with the ceiling fan in our room?" They dragged the study table under the fan and placed a chair on top. Arj climbed up and gently unscrewed a couple of screws. He felt around for a gasket on the base plate and pried it loose with the tip of the screwdriver. He climbed down and turned on the fan. It began rotating slowly, making a horrendous noise, like nails being run over a blackboard.

Tam and Mira screamed. "Enough! Turn it off!"

Arj grinned. "I guess we need a Fan-Fixer."

He rang Fan-Fixer Faekku, who promised to come the next day.

At around half past eleven, Tam was scouring the yard, looking for fallen mangoes, when she heard someone talking to Dumdumchechi in the cowshed. Tam made her way to a window and peered in. Someone was shouting at Dumdumchechi. His back was to Tam, and she couldn't see who it was. Dumdumchechi looked terrified. At one point, he even raised his hand as if he were going to hit her. Dumdumchechi lifted her arms to protect herself.

Tam didn't want Dumdumchechi to come to harm. She called out her name, waited a few seconds, and walked into the cowshed. She saw the curtain at the end of the room move.

The angry man was gone.

"Can you help me pluck some mangoes? They are too high up on the tree for me."

Dumdumchechi seemed relieved to escape the cowshed. After they plucked a few mangoes, Tam had to leave.

"I'll be back in ten minutes with some raw mango pickle." She didn't want the angry man to get any ideas when she was away. She ran to the kitchen and handed Pitamma the mangoes. By then, Fan-Fixer Faekku had arrived to fix the broken fan.

Fan-Fixer Faekku asked the children to help him pull the desk to the center of the room. He leaped on top of the desk and examined the fan. "Two screws are missing, and a gasket seems to have fallen off. That is what is making the noise."

The three of them nodded, pretending to be amazed that Fan-Fixer Faekku had figured out why the fan was making a racket.

"Wow!"

"You are so clever."

"How did you know?"

Fan-Fixer Faekku grinned. He shrugged. "It's my job." He fixed the fan in under half an hour. "My charge is one hun-hun-hundred rupees, parts and labor included. I usually charge m-m-more, but I have given you a small discount."

"We don't have the money now, but I can come by your shop tomorrow to pay you," Arj replied.

A look of anger flashed on Fan-Fixer Faekku's face. He controlled his features and set his face in a tight smile. "I have a new shop on Maidan Road, past Gelf Bakery. You can come by anytime after ten o'clock in the morning."

Arj nodded. As soon as Faekku left, the detectives high-fived each other.

"Yes!" said Arj, pleased. "We will have access to the shop tomorrow. I also want to check out that Gelf Bakery. I've heard the honey cakes are delicious."

The next day, the kids headed for Fan-Fixer Faekku's shop around three o'clock in the afternoon. Tam filled her cousins in about the incident at the cowshed.

Arj pedaled furiously, with Mira perched at the back of his bike. When they passed Gelf Bakery, Arj stopped, panting hard.

"Mira, you look small and light, but you are heavier than a rhinoceros. I need something to drink, or I will die."

The kids circled back to the bakery and ordered a puff, two honey cakes, and a lemon soda each. Gorging on the goodies, they plotted to get Fan-Fixer Faekku away from his shop. Arj had an idea.

"Tam, you stay here. In fifteen minutes, call Fan-Fixer Faekku and tell him the fridge at Gelf Bakery has broken down. With him on his way here, Mira and I can search his store."

Fan-Fixer Faekku seemed pleased to see Mira and Arj. His "shop" was a small shed crammed with old electrical equipment—TVs, ACs, radios, tape-recorders, and all sorts of wires. An assortment of odd screws littered the floor. Fan-Fixer Faekku wasn't very organized.

"I opened this shop last week. I have paid the rent in full for a year without borrowing a pai-pai-paisa from anybody," he said with pride. He seemed like he had more to say, but the phone in the shop rang. He picked it up, yes-yesed, and put it down.

He looked at Arj and Mira. "I need a favor. Can you mind the shop for half an hour? I have to rush to Gelf Bakery to fix a fridge. Normally, I would have locked up, but today a customer is supposed to drop off his AC. It is bad for business if he finds the shop closed."

Arj and Mira couldn't believe their luck. They nodded, trying not to look too enthusiastic.

After Fan-Fixer Faekku left, Arj turned to Mira. "Stand by the door. When you see him coming back, whistle." Then he began to search the shop methodically. He looked under the ACs, radios, and TVs. There was nothing there. He spotted an unlocked desk drawer, the key hanging in the lock. Inside, Arj found some cash and a calculator but no gold. He checked the shelves, lifted everything that could be lifted, investigated every bag, box, and envelope in that room—nothing. He was exhausted.

Mira gave a single low whistle. Arj immediately stopped his search for the jewelry and sat down on a chair. He gave the shop one last anxious look. It was such a mess—even if Arj had moved things around, Fan-Fixer Faekku could never tell.

Fan-Fixer Faekku returned, looking very unhappy. "Some time-wasting, jobless fool played a prank on me. There was no fridge trouble at Gelf Bakery."

Mira felt guilty about setting him up and said, "Maybe they are jealous of your success."

That got him to smile. "True! People were surprised when I opened this shop. I am the first person in three generations to run a business. Everyone in our family has always worked for someone else."

Arj and Mira went back to the bakery. They found Tam bingeing on cream puffs and giggling.

"Fan-Fixer Faekku was so angry! He yelled at the people in the bakery. Did you find anything?" Arj and Mira shook their heads.

They didn't know what else to do. The kids rode home, feeling like failed detectives.

"Should we ask Thombu? Maybe he has discovered an alibi for Fan-Fixer Faekku for the night of the burglary?" asked Tam.

Arj looked grim. "I am not sure if Thombu will help us, but it's worth a try. Tam, you could check out Fan-Fixer Faekku's house in the meantime. I found the address from the shop. Mira and I will speak to Thombu."

Thombu was thrilled to see them. He showed off his medals—silver for the egg-and-spoon race in the Elathoor Police Annual Picnic; and gold for table tennis (Damodar Ammavan had laughed about it, claiming Thombu had won because no one else in Elathoor could even play).

Thombu organized some files on the desk and asked an assistant to take them away. He then ordered a constable to offer the kids juice. After establishing his importance at the police station, he looked at Mira and Arj, his eyes glittering with curiosity.

"What can this humble government servant do for you?"

Arj confided in Thombu. "We have reason to suspect Fan-Fixer Faekku. We were wondering if you had investigated him. Does he have an alibi for the night of the burglary?"

Thombu lost his cool. "Are you questioning my abilities? Of course I checked out Fan-Fixer Faekku. He claimed he was with his mother the night of the burglary and that I was free to question her anytime I wanted. Detective work isn't for children. Not everyone has the training that I do. I will let this visit of yours slide, but the next time you come in here asking questions about the investigation, I will let your parents know."

Mira and Arj nodded meekly. Arj had an inkling that Thombu might be uncooperative, but his outburst didn't matter. They got what they needed—Fan-Fixer Faekku's alibi. They said their goodbyes and made their way out.

Arj looked at Mira. "I don't think Thombu questioned Faekku's mother, do you?"

Meanwhile, Tam looked for Fan-Fixer Faekku's house using Arj's directions. As she cycled down a mud path in Fan-Fixer Faekku's neighborhood, she noticed the houses there didn't have proper roofs or walls; they were huts topped with straw. Tam spotted an old man seated in front of a tea shop, reading a newspaper. She got off her bike.

"Chetta, may I have some tea?"

The tea shop owner was curious about who she was and why she was in the neighborhood on her own. When she told him, his attitude changed from curious to courteous. He told her what a great man her uncle was and gave her a free biscuit with tea. She then asked him if he knew where Fan-Fixer Faekku lived.

At the mention of Fan-Fixer Faekku's name, the old man on the bench lowered his newspaper. "That scoundrel worked with me for five years. He learned everything he could from me, and now he has opened up a shop right across from mine! I am losing customers to him." He spat on the ground in anger. "Why couldn't that son of a brinjal set up shop farther away and not eat into his teacher's trade? The problem with young people today is that they have no respect for their elders. All they do is chase after money." He glared at Tam, daring her to say something.

Tam shifted uncomfortably. "Where did he get the money to set up shop in the first place?"

The tea shop owner joined in the conversation. "Fan-Fixer Faekku's mother died, and he inherited her jewelry."

The old man bitterly remarked, "I won't be surprised if he killed his mother for the gold."

"Did you know his mother? Did she live with him?" Tam asked.

"He used to live alone. Two weeks ago, he told everyone in the neighborhood his mother had passed away. Then, a week ago, he claimed he had inherited her jewelry, some of which he sold and set up the shop with the money from the sale."

Tam finished her tea and biscuit. "Could you point out his house, please? I have to ask him to fix something at Lili Villa."

It was the fourth house down from the tea shop. Tam called out for him from outside—no one answered. She looked around; the street was empty. Then, Tam noticed the door was unlocked. She pushed it open and confidently walked in.

Inside, Tam saw a cot piled high with crumpled bedsheets. Below the cot was a trunk. It reminded her of Mira's description of Dumdumchechi's room.

She began frantically searching the place. There were so few places to hide anything that the search hardly took a few minutes. Finally, she opened the trunk and found some clothes, two bottles of brandy, an old cell phone, and, right at the bottom, two small photographs. The pictures looked oddly familiar. Tam slipped them into her back pocket. *Arj might recognize the people in the photo. He's good with stuff like that.*

She walked out of Fan-Fixer Faekku's hut and sighed in relief. The street was still empty. She got on Mira's bike and raced home, the photographs burning a hole in her back pocket.

At Lili Villa, Arj and Mira were stuffing their faces with sweet kozhukkatta.

Tam popped them into her mouth two at a time. "Detective work makes you hungry."

After she gobbled a few more, they compared notes. Arj was excited. "Fan-Fixer Faekku lied! He couldn't have been with his mother on the night of the burglary if she had passed away by then. And, if he only sold some of Amma's jewels to rent the shop, he would still have some left over. If he is guilty, he must either have a LOT of money stashed away somewhere, or he still has the jewelry on him."

Tam remembered the photographs she had pinched and pulled them out. Arj stared at them for a while. Then he whispered something in Mira's and Tam's ears.

Tam yelled, "This means Fan-Fixer Faekku is the thief! These photographs explain everything!"

Arj calmed her down. "We still need proof. Where could he have stashed the loot? We need to find it to prove his guilt."

THIRTEEN

THE DANGER OF SLEUTHING AT NIGHT

Arj, Tam, and Mira were unusually quiet, thinking hard of ways to prove Fan-Fixer Faekku's guilt. It was a horrible feeling to know something to be true and yet have nothing to convince the world. They contemplated going to Thombu, but the policeman had been unfriendly, and his abilities as a detective didn't inspire their confidence.

"I didn't check the roof at Fan-Fixer Faekku's hut. Do you think he wove the gold into the straw?" Mira and Arj looked at Tam in disbelief.

"What?" Tam shrugged. "In this book I'm reading, gold is sewn into a lady's dress."

Arj shook his head. "I don't think he will risk leaving it at home. It must be somewhere else, somewhere right under our noses. We are missing an obvious place."

After another half hour of silence, Tam yelled, "I can't take it anymore! I want chocolate. I need chocolate, or I will explode!"

Arj and Mira stared at their strange cousin. "Hello! You are not in Bengaluru. This is Elathoor. It's eight o'clock at night, and all the shops are shut."

"If I could get my hands on some chocolate right now, I am sure I can crack this case. I know the shops are closed. Would Pitamma have any chocolate?"

"Umm, no. But she might have some jaggery." Tam looked like she was about to cry.

Mira felt sorry for her cousin. When Tam wanted something, she had to get it NOW, or she would sulk and moan till she got it.

Mira sighed. "Close your eyes, both of you."

She walked to her closet. "No peeking!" After checking on Arj and Tam, Mira opened the door and brought out her grandma's old cassette player. It was ancient, the kind that played music from an audio cassette. Mira opened the battery compartment. There, instead of batteries, Mira had stashed away three miniature chocolate bars. Curious, Arj and Tam took a quick peek before she looked up. Poor Mira, she would have to think of another hiding place—every time Arj was hungry (which was frequently), he would now raid her stash.

The bars were a bit gooey from being trapped inside the player for so long, but the kids didn't mind. Arj licked the wrapper to get every last bit of chocolate when something struck him. He had an idea.

"We have to go back to Fan-Fixer Faekku's shop tomorrow." He refused to tell the girls why.

"Trust me, I will explain later. But first, we need something we can take to his shop for repairs."

Mira held up the player.

"Do you have one of those old-fashioned cassettes?"

Mira nodded and took out two from inside the closet. Tam had never seen one of these things and looked at them in wonder. They looked fascinating, with transparent bodies and spools of tightly wound tape.

Arj plugged the player into a socket, inserted a cassette, and pressed play. An old Malayalam song filled the room. Arj pressed the pause button and then fast-forwarded. Pause, fast-forward, pause, fast-forward, pause, fast-forward—he repeated this cycle many times over, the old steel buttons clicking into place with a distinctive tuk-tuk sound. After a while, the cassette jammed in the player. They tried pulling it out, but the tape was caught in the mechanism.

"Now we have a problem that Fan-Fixer Faekku has to fix!"

The next day, the three of them set off with the cassette player to Fan-Fixer Faekku's shop. He seemed quite pleased to see them. He liked having regular customers.

Mira handed him the jammed player. Fan-Fixer Faekku peered inside the cassette compartment.

"Ah! Not a problem. I can fix this in a few minutes."

He used a screwdriver to pry the tape loose. Then, he rewound the tape using the back of the screwdriver.

"You know, I used to know your grandma when I was young. She would always give me something to eat whenever I came over to Lili Villa to play. She was so kind. Every time I visit your house now, I think about her." Arj was curious. He was sure his parents had never mentioned Fan-Fixer Faekku visiting the house as a child.

The trip down memory lane seemed to have softened Fan-Fixer Faekku. He was eager to help.

"The cassette head is dirty and will cause problems later. I can clean it in a few minutes if you kids can wait." He stepped out to get some cleaning liquid from a hardware store down the road, asking them to mind the shop.

Arj dashed to the other end and undid both the bolts on the back door as soon as he left. You couldn't tell the door was unbolted—they were black bolts on a black door. Arj hoped Fan-Fixer Faekku wouldn't notice that his door was unlocked.

Fan-Fixer Faekku was apologetic when he returned. "The store is out of cleaning liquid. If you leave the player behind, I can clean it and bring it over to Lili Villa for n-n-no charge." They thanked him and walked out, trying not to stare at the back door.

"No, no, NO!" Arj was firm, but Mira begged him piteously. She had said a million pleases, but he was adamant. "I wish I didn't have to ask Tam either, but two heads are better than one. Also, we cannot take your bike, Mira. It is bright pink and glows at night."

He had explained this many times to Mira, but she refused to see the logic. Finally, he stopped trying to convince her. They would have to leave her behind. Arj would take the keys to her bike to make sure she didn't get any funny ideas.

He went over the plan again. "Tam and I will sneak out of the house at one o'clock tonight. It's a twenty-minute ride to Fan-Fixer Faekku's shop. We will be dressed in black tees and black shorts to blend into the darkness."

He pulled out a flashlight from his desk and packed a black knapsack with sandwiches and a flask of Bournvita. He couldn't take his little sister, even if a part of him felt bad about leaving her behind. This adventure could be dangerous. If he weren't afraid of being ridiculed by Tam and Mira, he would have confessed the whole thing to his parents and let them handle it.

The children were so quiet over their mutton-curry-and-chapati dinner that Sheila Ammayi took their temperatures. After the meal, they silently trooped to their room. The joyful ruckus they usually created in the evening was absent.

Tam was scared, Arj anxious, and poor Mira was unhappy and angry at being left out.

That night, they couldn't sleep. When the clock struck half past twelve, Arj washed his face and brushed his teeth.

"I always feel more alert when I brush my teeth. I think it's the mint in the toothpaste."

Tam followed suit, and so did Mira. She explained, "I will stay awake until you come back. If you don't come home by six, I will wake Appa and Amma up."

"That is a good idea, Mira," said Arj. "If anything goes wrong, you can bring help."

Tam gulped. "This feels so scary. I don't know whether to laugh or cry."

At one o'clock, they sneaked out. Arj unlocked his bike and wheeled it to the gate. Lili Villa's gate was squeaky, and the kids didn't want to take any chances: they had left it ajar after dinner.

Just outside the gate, they heard an agonized mewl. Tam yelped in fear. It was Whisko darting into the yard— Arj had run over the poor thing's tail with his bike. The cousins froze, too scared to even whisper. Lili Villa stayed dark. After what felt like forever, Arj pushed his bicycle through the gates, with Tam following silently.

Once outside, they were able to breathe more freely. A cool breeze fanned their faces, and the moon was bright enough to light their way. There wasn't a soul on the street.

Tam grinned at Arj. It was a real adventure! Arj got on his bike, and Tam perched herself on the back. They were on one of the most thrilling rides of their lives. It felt like they owned the whole wide world.

Turning a corner, they spotted a policeman on his beat, patrolling the streets while rhythmically tapping his lathi stick on the ground. Arj knew there would be trouble if he spotted them. They quickly got off the bike and looked around. Tam nudged Arj and jerked her head to the left.

There was a large delivery truck parked up ahead. They stashed the bike behind the truck and found a spot to hide. The kids stood still, merging with the shadows in the dark. After a while, they could hear the policeman's footsteps fading away and the tap-tap-tap of his lathi growing fainter.

They waited to make sure he didn't return. The sounds grew softer and vanished into the night. Arj peeked from behind the truck. The road was clear.

Arj pedaled as fast as he could to Fan-Fixer Faekku's shop, his heart loudly drumming in his chest. They reached the shop in record time. The kids parked the bike against a wall and went around the shop to the back door. Arj sent up a silent prayer and pushed against it. The door swung open, revealing a dark abyss. It was like walking into a cave.

Tam and Arj stepped into the darkness and closed the door behind them. After a few minutes, their eyes got used to the low light, and they could make out the shapes that dotted the shop—ACs, television sets, radios, and an odd toolbox or two.

Tam opened a window to let in some moonlight, and the detectives set to work. They carefully opened the backs of air conditioners and television sets. Since most of them had already been unscrewed by Fan-Fixer Faekku, it wasn't too hard.

After an hour, Arj had to admit he was wrong. "The jewelry is not hidden in this shop. When Mira took out those chocolates from her hiding place, I was convinced Fan-Fixer Faekku was hiding the gold inside the equipment for repair. What do we do now?"

Both of them slid down to the dusty floor, feeling defeated. Tam absentmindedly fiddled with Mira's cassette player, pressing stop and play alternatively. The tuk-tuk sound of the buttons felt reassuring in the silence. Tam idly wondered if Mira had refilled her chocolate stash before they brought the player in for repair. She opened the battery compartment again.

"Gosh!" she whispered. "Look! Look!"

Hidden inside the battery box was Sheila Ammayi's gold jewelry, glittering in the moonlight.

The kids were so stunned that they didn't react for a few minutes. Then Arj whooped in joy. "I was right!"

The gravity of the situation hit him. "We have to head home immediately and let Appa know. We should probably leave the cassette player and the jewelry behind for Thombu. It's proof of Fan-Fixer Faekku's guilt."

They stood up, dusted their backsides, and began to walk toward the back door. Suddenly, they heard the unmistakable sound of a key turning in a lock. Arj rushed to the door and tried to pull it open. It held firm. They were locked in.

Tam looked up at the window. It had iron bars; they couldn't crawl out through the window. The roof was too high.

She let out a sob. "We will probably be killed in this stuffy room, and our bodies will be thrown into the Elathoor river, weighed down with stones. Nobody will find us."

Arj put his arm over her shoulder. For the first time since the adventure began, he felt like a child in a world full of cruel grown-ups. He picked up an iron rod and balanced it on his shoulder. "If anyone tries to hurt us, they will have to get past me first. I'll buy you time to escape, Tam."

Tam was about to get all sappy and say something like she would never leave him behind, when a light shone through the window. They instinctively ducked. The beam trailed around the room, missing them by a few inches.

A terrified voice whispered, "Tam. . . Arj, are you there?"

"Mira!"

Mira couldn't bear being left behind and had followed them. Arj had forgotten about the spare keys to her bike, which she had hidden away in their piggy bank.

"I am so glad to hear your voice! How brave you are to cycle all the way here on your own! Even I wouldn't have done that."

Tam quickly brought Mira up to speed. "We found Sheila Ammayi's jewelry—it was hidden in the back of your cassette player! Someone locked us in here. Can you run to the back door and see if you can let us out?"

Tam and Arj could hear Mira tugging at the door from the other side. Whoever had locked them in had taken the key with them.

"Forget the door, Mira," Arj called out to her. "Rush home and tell Appa and Amma."

Though she knew what Tam and Arj would say, Mira asked in a small voice, "Can't one of you come with me?"

"You are on your own, Mira. You know the way—head straight for home. Don't worry, Elathoor is a very safe place. And, Mira, no matter what you see, *don't stop* until you reach Lili Villa."

Mira got on her bike and whizzed off. Tam wished she were the one doing the rescuing.

Arj prayed Mira would bring help before the mysterious person with the key returned. For now, there was nothing Arj and Tam could do. They waited in the dark, their fears wrapped around them like a tight blanket.

FOURTEEN

THE RESCUER MAY NEED RESCUING

Mira's hands were shaking. She stopped and took ten deep breaths to calm down. She dug out her bicycle key and turned it in the lock. *Click.* The sound felt like an explosion in the silence. She looked around fearfully. There was no one around.

Mira pedaled as fast as she could. A few minutes later, she heard footsteps behind her—someone was following her. She looked over her shoulder and cried out in fear.

A dark shadow loomed over her. A passing cloud had blocked the moon, and she couldn't make out a face. She pedaled furiously, but it was a little bike, and it could only go so fast. Mira turned the corner and shot a quick look behind her. Whoever was following her had vanished. She looked back to find the shadow running alongside, breathing hard to keep up with her. Mira desperately tried to think of something to protect herself with. There was nothing she could spot. The street looked desolate in the moonlight.

Mira began to sweat. She could see Lili Villa in the distance, but it was not close enough yet. Even if she screamed, her parents wouldn't be able to hear her. Then, suddenly, her bike refused to move. No matter how hard she pedaled, she stayed put. Someone was pulling her back.

She couldn't cry out; her throat had gone dry. Tears streamed down her cheeks. She turned around to see who it was.

A wild-looking man stood behind her. His clothes were torn, his hair hung in clumps, unwashed and stringy. His eyes were red. He grinned at Mira, baring his yellow teeth.

Mira sighed in relief. It was Pottan.

No one knew Pottan's real name or where he came from. He roamed the streets of Elathoor, appearing and disappearing at will. He would often turn up at people's homes at mealtimes. Pitamma always had something for him. She told Mira once, "He is not well. We should always treat him with kindness." Villagers would give him new clothes to wear all the time, but he would always end up dressed in rags. Perhaps he tore his clothes in his sleep.

Pottan was like a child. He had never hurt anyone or anything in his life. He must have thought chasing Mira was a game. The only way to get rid of Pottan was to look at him, hold two fingers up, wiggle them, and then scratch your nose with those two fingers. For some reason, this gesture terrified him.

Smiling through her tears, Mira held up her fingers, wiggled them, and then deliberately scratched her nose. He immediately released her bike, turned around, and ran away. Mira gulped. She had never been so scared in her entire life. She got back on the bike and raced home. Once Mira reached Lili Villa, she held on to the gate with both hands. She was okay. If she screamed now, her parents would be able to hear her.

FIFTEEN

A RESCUE IS EXECUTED
AND THE GUILTY TRICKED

Mira pushed the gate. It swung open, creaking like a train grinding to a halt. She didn't care about the racket she was making. Whisko came up to her and rubbed against her leg, as if to say, "You are safe now." She scratched his ear. The lights in her parents' room came on. Mira threw her bike aside, rushed to the front door, and kept ringing the bell until the door opened.

She fell into her father's arms, tears streaming down her face. She began to hiccup from crying. Sheila Ammayi carried her in, sat her on her lap, and held her. When the hiccups subsided, Mira quickly narrated all that had happened.

Damodar Ammavan was about to ask a million questions, but Sheila Ammayi stopped him.

"Let's get the children home safe, and then we can listen to the entire story."

Pitamma appeared as if by magic and made cups of hot

chocolate for everyone. Mira thought of Tam and Arj alone in that dark room without any chocolate, and tears began rolling down her cheeks again.

Damodar Ammavan called Thombu. He arrived at Lili Villa in under ten minutes. After hearing a brief explanation, Thombu's eyebrows shot up.

"How? When? Why? Who?"

"Thombu, we need to get the children back home." Damodar Ammavan rushed him out. "They will answer all your questions later." Thombu wasn't satisfied, but he listened to his friend.

The two men jumped into a police jeep and set off toward Fan-Fixer Faekku's shop. Mira begged them to take her along, but she wasn't allowed to go. A part of her was secretly relieved. She had had enough adventures for one night. She cuddled up to her amma on the sofa and waited for Tam and Arj. She missed them so much.

Thombu radioed the police station. "Send two armed constables to Fan-Fixer Faekku's shop. Ask them to meet us outside."

Turning onto Maidan Road, Thombu turned off the headlights and killed the engine. The jeep glided down a slope. Thombu brought it to a stop a few feet in front of the shop. Damodar Ammavan felt an unpleasant fear building up as they neared the front door. He thought about the kids locked up in the shop, all alone in the dark.

Arj and Tam had been waiting for what seemed like forever.

"I hope Mira is okay. What if someone hurts her? She is so tiny. I wish I hadn't sent her alone. I should have just told Appa, and he would have handled this whole thing. We were foolish to think we could do this by ourselves."

Tam scowled at Arj. She hoped he wouldn't start to cry, especially when she had so many gloomy thoughts herself. *What if the person who had locked them in came back, captured them, and sold them to a circus, where she and Arj would have to shovel elephant poo for the rest of their lives?*

Thombu and Damodar Ammavan had been so quiet that Arj and Tam didn't even realize that help was outside. Thombu flashed a light through the window and called out, "Are you kids in there?"

"Yes, yes, YES!" Arj and Tam jumped up and began waving frantically, as if they were being rescued from a shipwreck on a remote island. They never dreamed that a day would come when they would be glad to see Thombu!

"Mira got home safe!" exclaimed Arj in sheer relief.

Damodar Ammavan and Thombu rushed to the front door. Damodar Ammavan was getting ready to kick the door in when Thombu held him back.

"Wait."

He pulled out an enormous bunch of keys and patiently tried fitting one key at a time into the keyhole.

The fifteenth key clicked, and it turned perfectly to open the door.

Arj and Tam raced to hug Damodar Ammavan. They even thanked Thombu. At that moment, they would have gladly kissed him on both cheeks. They led the grown-ups to the gold and explained how they had found it.

Thombu listened carefully.

"Are you going to arrest him now?" Arj asked.

Thombu shook his head. "If we arrest him right now, he can claim you planted the jewelry in the cassette player. He will say he didn't even know it was there. We need to trick him into admitting his guilt."

"How?"

Thombu snapped his fingers; he had an idea. He whispered in Damodar Ammavan's ear.

Damodar Ammavan called Fan-Fixer Faekku and spoke in a low voice. "Hello, I am calling from the fire department. We received a call notifying us of a fire at 62 Maidan Road. Is that your shop?"

They could hear Fan-Fixer Faekku screaming, "Yes, yes, that is my address! Oh, please save my shop! I have expensive equipment there. I am on my way. I am comin—" His voice cut out.

Thombu locked up the shop. By then, two constables had joined them, and Thombu gave them instructions.

"Damu, you and Constable Ravi will guard the back door while Constable Rajiv and I will hide behind this tree. Children, could you please hide in those bushes there? I don't want you involved in this operation."

It wasn't long before they spotted Fan-Fixer Faekku pedaling as fast as he could. He leaped off his bike in front of the shop, not noticing the police jeep parked nearby. He looked around suspiciously. He didn't understand—the store wasn't on fire.

Faekku looked at his phone. "Someone called me eight minutes ago." He walked up to the shop and unlocked the door. He turned on the lights and looked around, his thoughts racing. *Everything seems to be just as I left it. No! Not everything. What is this flask doing here? It smells of Bournvita. Who could be drinking milk in my shop?*

He scanned the room for intruders, and then he rushed to the cassette player and popped the battery compartment. The gold was still there. Relieved, he decided to carry the jewelry with him. He couldn't risk leaving it behind after that strange phone call.

He turned around to see a grinning sub-inspector and two constables waiting for him. Thombu, as if he were in a movie, held up the handcuffs so that they caught the moonlight and shimmered.

They had caught him red-handed!

Fan-Fixer Faekku turned around and tried escaping through the back door. He ran straight into Damodar Ammavan's arms, who held him in a tight grip till he was handcuffed.

Much to his surprise, Fan-Fixer Faekku spotted Tam and Arj crawling out from behind a bush. Everyone squeezed into the jeep—Tam and Arj sat in the back while the two constables crushed Fan-Fixer Faekku between them. He was puzzled, wondering why they were there. Naturally, he couldn't ask. The kids tried not to smile. This was exciting!

Thombu dropped off Dr. Damodar and his family at Lili Villa. "I have to take the jewelry to the station first to complete some paperwork. I'll bring it back in an hour."

"The children are safe. You can bring back the gold whenever you want." The jeep whizzed off, taking the thief to jail.

Mira rushed out to meet them. Tam and Arj grinned from ear to ear. They yelled, "Group hug!" and they held each other tight.

"We are the best detectives in the world!" Tam whispered.

It was four o'clock in the morning, but everyone was too wired to go to bed. The family sat around the dining table, and Pitamma plied them with cups of black tea, banana chips, and carrot cake. It felt like a party.

Mira, Tam, and Arj told Damodar Ammavan and Sheila Ammayi everything—how they had investigated each suspect, the places they explored, and the secrets they uncover. Every little detail.

When Damodar Ammavan heard about the rope to the roof from Dumdumchechi's secret room, he was furious. He asked Pitamma to wake her up and bring her to the house.

Pitamma returned in less than five minutes. "There is no one living above the cowshed. The suitcase, clothes, and kitchen utensils Mira described are all gone."

Dumdumchechi had left without letting anyone know. Damodar Ammavan looked puzzled.

"Her disappearance makes her look guilty, but how is she connected to Fan-Fixer Faekku?"

Tam jumped up. "I have a clue!" She brought out the photographs she had taken from Fan-Fixer Faekku's house. One of them was a small black-and-white photo of cows—Dumdumchechi's beloved cows. The other photo showed a little boy standing in front of Lili Villa with a much younger Dumdumchechi.

Sheila Ammayi broke the silence. "Fan-Fixer Faekku is Velu, Dumdumchechi's son! I remember him now—he used to play at Lili Villa as a child."

The sky was turning orange. Thombu dropped in, looking extremely satisfied with himself. Pitamma handed him a cup of black tea. He took a sip. It was perfect. She flashed him a paan-stained smile. She had forgiven him for investigating her. After all, he had saved her children.

After a few sips of the refreshing brew, he announced, "Fan-Fixer Faekku has made a full confession. He is the one who stole your jewelry with the help of his mother, Dumdumchechi." No one looked surprised, which annoyed Thombu. He continued, "Naturally, we caught her as well. There was no way she could escape the far-reaching hands of the law."

He handed Sheila Ammayi a bag. "Please check the contents carefully. That scoundrel Fan-Fixer Faekku sold some of it to a traveling goldsmith. He didn't even know the goldsmith's name. I don't think we will be able to recover it."

Sheila Ammayi looked through the bundle and smiled for the first time that night. "A necklace and a pair of earrings are missing, but it doesn't matter. I didn't expect to get this much back."

Thombu bristled. "You didn't trust the police to be able to crack this case?"

Before Sheila Ammayi could reply, Pitamma cackled, "What police? It was the children who solved this mystery!"

Damodar Ammavan tried not to smile. He changed the subject. "We are not going to keep our gold at home, Sheila.

As soon as the bank opens today, we are going to put it in a safe."

Tam stomped her foot and demanded, "What happened exactly? How did Fan-Fixer Faekku steal the jewels?"

Thombu grinned. He was waiting for someone to ask. With six pairs of eyes trained on him, he felt important. He pulled out his new phone. "I recorded Fan-Fixer Faekku's confession. Would you like to hear it?"

"Yes, please! Please! Pretty please!"

Thombu pressed play, and Fan-Fixer Faekku's voice filled the room.

SIXTEEN

HOW TO BUNGLE A BURGLARY

My real name is Velu, and I broke my mother's heart. My mother, Dumdumchechi (as you call her), didn't want to steal from the good doctors, but I forced her to. I told her if she wouldn't help me, she would never see me again.

When a ceiling fan in Dr. Damodar's house developed a problem, I saw an opportunity. Under the pretext of fixing the fan, I removed a rubber gasket so that it would make an awful racket, ensuring the doctors wouldn't be able to hear a thing over the noise.

At one o'clock on the night of the twelfth, I walked to Lili Villa. I didn't need a flashlight because I knew the way well. I could sense every stone and tree; I played there as a child.

I saw Kodavis gathering some trash, and I waited until he left. Everyone inside the house was asleep. I climbed onto the roof using the mango tree as a ladder and walked over to the side across from my mother's room.

She was standing at the window, looking sad and scared. I threw a rope at her, which she dropped two times. Clumsy! On the third try, she caught the rope and tied it to her window bar.

I tied the other end to the roof and looked around—no one was awake. I found the spot on the roof right above the doctors' room. I removed some of the tiles, tied another rope to the wooden beam below, and slid down into their room.

The doctors were fast asleep, snoring in different rhythms. I tiptoed to the steel closet; it was unlocked. The gold lay there glistening, asking me to take it. The doctors had enough money; they didn't need the jewelry as much as I did. I filled a little bag with the jewels and climbed up onto the roof. I quickly walked across the roof and slid the bag of jewels to my mother.

I was like a cat: lithe, silent, and sure-footed. Nobody heard a thing.

Before leaving, I used a pair of Dr. Damodar's shoes to leave footprints on the walls. I let go of the rope and jumped down with a thud. Then, I made some more footprints on the ground. I knew Sub-Inspector Thombu would investigate the burglary. Once he discovered the print in the doctor's size, it would confuse him and give me more time to sell the gold. I got lucky—not only did it match the doctor's shoe, but it also fit Kodavis, Pitamma, Thombu, and my mother.

How I laughed when she told me about the mix-up! Back at my mother's room, we opened the bag. There was enough to make our dreams come true. My mother would finally be able to buy back her cows, and I could open up a repair shop. In our excitement, we forgot to untie the rope.

A few days later, I heard from my mother that Mira was spending a lot of time in the cowshed, and I was worried she would discover the secret room. My mother had assured me that Mira was too much of a scaredy-cat to snoop around.

I didn't want to split the gold with my mother. I think she knew that I wouldn't keep my promise to her, so she decided to steal from me on the very night the Lili Villa kids were snooping around in my shop. She heard their voices inside and knew our game was up. She was the one who locked them in. My mother ran off to catch a train to get away from Elathoor. But she got caught! Sub-Inspector Thombu had sent her photograph to the railway officials. The minute she got off the train, they recognized her and handcuffed her. Serves her right—who steals from their son?

Now we are both in jail. On some days, I wish I had been a better son. On other days, I wish she had been a better mother. Perhaps then, we could have both escaped.

SEVENTEEN

THE TERRIFIC THREE

Tam's mother arrived at Lili Villa holding a suitcase in one hand and a newspaper in the other.

"Tam, I let you off the hook for a few weeks, and you manage to get yourself on the front page of the local paper. How do you do it?"

Tam rushed up to her and gave her a big hug. She glanced at the paper and yelled, "Arj, Mira! Come here!"

The kids crowded around the paper. There was a story about them on the front page!

The Times of Elathoor

Your news. Local news. Best news.

www.thetimesofelathoor.com

Three to Catch a Thief

Staff Reporter

Elathoor—May 29th

Last night, Sub-Inspector Thombu Illayath arrested a man suspected of a burglary that took place at Lili Villa, the home of our reputed village doctors. The suspect, known locally as Fan-Fixer Faekku, was caught with the jewelry on his person. He has since confessed to the crime.

Sub-Inspector Thombu showed quick thinking in capturing the criminal and his accomplice. The police received help in cracking the case from an unlikely source: three children. Arjun Damodar (11), Mira Damodar (9), and Tamara Menon (10) helped solve the mystery by displaying some smart sleuthing skills and incredible courage. They investigated seven suspects and zeroed in on Fan-Fixer Faekku to find the jewelry hidden inside his shop on Maidan Road.

The suspects are currently in jail, and the jewelry has been returned to the family.

The Times of Elathoor *salutes the three children for their bravery. They are an inspiration, not just to children everywhere, but to us all. They are truly the Terrific Three!*

Sheila Ammayi looked up from her copy of the paper and smiled. "'The Terrific Three' has such a grand ring to it."

Pitamma made idiyappam and thenga pal to celebrate. It was so good that everyone stuffed themselves silly.

The kids settled into their room to read when Damodar Ammavan and Sheila Ammayi came looking for them.

They had a surprise for the trio—presents for solving the case and finding the jewelry. Arj got a new phone and Mira a pair of roller skates, which she thought were super cool.

As for Tam, her uncle and aunt asked her to step outside. There, shining bright in the sunlight, was a beautiful blue bike. She whooped in joy. She rode around the yard in circles.

"Yay! How lucky am I! I have two bikes now, one in Elathoor and one in Bengaluru!"

"Thombu has sent you a gift, too," Damodar Ammavan said, handing them a package. Inside were a pair of toy handcuffs, binoculars, and three pairs of gloves, along with a message: "To the best detectives in Elathoor—good luck for your future adventures."

Arj beamed. "That is sweet of him. He isn't all that bad."

The sun was beginning to set on the second-to-last day of their summer vacation. Tam and her mother were flying back to Bengaluru in the morning. She felt a bit sad that she had to leave, but she also couldn't wait to get back to school and boast about how she had solved a mystery!

Her thoughts were interrupted by Pitamma calling them for tea. Mira, who was already at the table, brought up something that had been bothering her.

"We never got a chance to investigate Veer Sagar. What was he doing at the house on the day of the burglary?"

They had forgotten about Veer Sagar.

As Chief Detective, Arj spoke up first. "He is, as of now, a mystery to solve, and we—"

Damodar Ammavan interrupted him, "We will get to it later. No fun in solving everything in a single summer, right?"

The detectives grinned and nodded. They were sure this wouldn't be their last adventure.

Tam suddenly remembered the girl who had been troubling Mira at school. She turned to Mira and said, "Let's go speak to that bully and set her straight."

Mira shook her head. "I am not scared anymore. I helped solve a case, remember? I can stand up for myself."

Tam whistled. She was impressed. Junior Chief Detective (Mira got that promotion!) could take care of herself.

FOOD FROM KERALA

Appam: A pancake made with fermented rice batter and coconut milk. Looks like a cap with a lace fringe.

Bilimbi: A green fruit, with a sharp, sour taste, that looks like a pickled gherkin.

Bournvita: Chocolate malt drink; makes you strong and keeps you awake. Not super-chocolatey, but yummy. Best had when studying for an exam or on an adventure.

Chapati (or Roti): A thin flatbread made of unleavened dough with dark brown bits like the craters on the moon.

Coconut Barfi: Dessert made with grated coconut and sugar. Bigger than a piece of chocolate but smaller than a smartphone.

Dosas: Round crepes made from a fermented rice and lentil batter. Ammas make it best.

Ginger Candy: Toffee made with ginger and sugar. One bite and your face will form the weirdest expressions.

Idiyappam: Rice noodles like thin worms all twisted and knotted together.

Jaggery: Rich and earthy form of sugar. Comes in the shape of golden-brown bricks. Ants will be happy if you build a house with it.

Kadala: Black chickpea curry, best eaten with puttu. A breakfast favorite in Kerala. You are allowed to smash a papadam into it.

Kozhukkatta: Little dumplings with a coconut-jaggery filling. Don't play catch with it. Just pop it in your mouth and swallow.

Masala: A mixture of ground spices, added to vegetables, meat, or rice. Usually fiery; keep a glass of water on standby.

Mutton Biryani: A delicacy made of rice and mutton. Tastes so good, even a goat would love to eat it. Baa!

Natholi: Anchovies. If you fry them, you can eat them whole. Crunch, crunch, crunch. They are better than chips.

Paan: Betel leaf with areca nut. Place in mouth, chew and spit, chew and spit. Stains your mouth just like a red lolly.

Papadam: Thin, crispy wafers that look like shiny mini frisbees.

Pazhampori: Banana fritters. You can't just eat one—when served, always ask for four or more.

Prasad: An offering served to devotees at a temple. You get a pinch but the taste packs a punch.

Puris: Puffy, deep-fried balls of unleavened bread, like oily spaceships. Delicious with potato curry.

Puttu: Rice flour layered with grated coconut and steamed in something that looks like a miniature chimney.

Roti (or Chapati): A thin flatbread made of unleavened dough with dark brown bits like the craters on the moon.

Sambar: Lentil stew with vegetables. Smells as good as it tastes. Slurp!

Stew: Gently spiced coconut-milk gravy with potato, carrots, and green peas. So delicious, you will have to go back for a second or third helping.

Thenga Pal: Coconut milk. Best with appam or idiyappam. Sweeten it with sugar, and you can drink a gallon.

Unnakkai: Steamed banana with coconut, fried in ghee. Looks like a butterfly cocoon but tastes way better.

Vadas: Savory donuts. Taste best with spicy coconut chutney. Do not try to eat the hole.

WORDS IN MALAYALAM AND HINDI

Amma: Mother, or She-Who-Must-Be-Obeyed

Ammavan: Uncle, or He-Who-Gets-Angry-For-Weird-Reasons

Ammayi: Aunt of the No-Means-No club

Appa: Father, or Softie-Who-Pretends-To-Be-Stern

Beedi: A cigarette—tobacco wrapped in a tendu leaf. It is terrible for your health.

Chappals: Rubber flip-flops, can be worn in every weather except snow. Expose your toes to the sun.

Chechi: An older sister. Also, any woman above fifty. Just don't ask how old she is. You may get into trouble.

Chetta: Brother. Also, any man whose name you don't know. When you have many chettas in the room, you can number them—Chetta 1, Chetta 2, Chetta 3. . . and so on.

Lungi: A piece of cloth tied around the lower half of the body. One tug and it comes right off.

Mallu: Another word for Malayali. These are the people who live in Kerala and speak a language called Malayalam.

Mundu-Veshti: A two-piece saree that Malayali women wear. Usually white or cream-colored with a gold border. Looks elegant but don't spill chutney on it.

Pooja: A Hindu ritual where you worship a deity with food and flowers.

Pujari: The person, usually a man, who performs pooja at a Hindu temple.

THANK YOU

Radhakrishnan Uncle and Shantichechi for love, and for making me feel their home was my home every single time I landed after taking overnight buses from god knows where.

Kala Sambasivan and Ambika Sambasivan for creating a beautiful, inclusive space like Yali Books, where the celebration of brown is authentic.

Ambika Sambasivan for being the publisher-editor that writers dream of—sensitive and intuitive with an absolute understanding of the heartbeat of the book.

Shruti Prabhu for a fabulous cover that captures summers in Kerala. Saraswathy Rajagopalan and Lisa Davis for their insightful editorial inputs.

My parents, P. Narayanankutty Menon, Krishnakumari, and my aunt Susheelchechi, who have always supported all my decisions, even the strange ones.

First readers, who ironed out niggles with more love than criticism—John, Kanchana, Zarine, Leela, Sreeja, Roopa, Ramu, Shruti, and Arthi.

My family in Kerala, who are always generous with their time, love, and good food—Ammuma, Velliachan, Rajaten, Padmachechi, Rajiv, Ravi, Poornima, Mincha, Radu, Ashokaten, Nishant, Vinodaten, Prematen, Venichechechi, Unni, Babuaten, Jayachechi, Arun, Anju, Rahul, Shordha, Anu, Lallichechi, Latha Teacher, Tallamma.

The next generation, who is my inspiration—Ashwini, Aditya, Lakshmi, Alvin, Rohan, Govind, Reesa, Arjun, Nandini, Aarnav, Madhav, Ethan, Meenakshi, and Gauri.

Rosalyn Ammai, who shone with kindness at a moment when it was needed.

Ahalya and Meethil of Trilogy Library, Mumbai, for their fantastic collection of children's books.

Mrs. Zarkies, the librarian of Sophia High School, Bengaluru, and Enid Blyton, for the gift of innumerable mystery books, which filled my childhood.

Sylvia Madrigal, who is always special.

DC Books (Mango), for publishing *A Thud in the Middle of the Night*.

The FAB Prize, UK, for believing that all writers need an extra pat on the back.

John, for love, and for always being an indefatigable cheerleader of all my dreams.

Kerala, for being the perfect summer vacation destination.

STAY TUNED FOR THE
NEXT ADVENTURE!

A TERRIFIC THREE MYSTERY
A MYSTERY AT THE MUMBAI TURF CLUB

CPSIA information can be obtained
at www.ICGtesting.com
Printed in the USA
LVHW091921061021
699707LV00008B/456/J

9 781949 52882